About the Author

Martin Matthews served in the Royal Marines and was a Firearms Officer in the police. Now retired, he is a trainer in the private security industry. Married and living in South Devon, he enjoys motorcycling and his retirement.

Cold Shot

Martin Matthews

Cold Shot

Olympia Publishers
London

www.olympiapublishers.com
OLYMPIA PAPERBACK EDITION

Copyright © Martin Matthews 2023

The right of Martin Matthews to be identified as author of
this work has been asserted in accordance with sections 77 and 78 of
the Copyright, Designs and Patents Act 1988.

All Rights Reserved

No reproduction, copy or transmission of this publication
may be made without written permission.
No paragraph of this publication may be reproduced,
copied or transmitted save with the written permission of the publisher,
or in accordance with the provisions
of the Copyright Act 1956 (as amended).

Any person who commits any unauthorised act in relation to
this publication may be liable to criminal
prosecution and civil claims for damage.

A CIP catalogue record for this title is
available from the British Library.

ISBN: 978-1-80439-568-4

This is a work of fiction.
Names, characters, places and incidents originate from the writer's
imagination. Any resemblance to actual persons, living or dead, is
purely coincidental.

First Published in 2023

Olympia Publishers
Tallis House
2 Tallis Street
London
EC4Y 0AB

Printed in Great Britain

Dedication

Dedicated to all those Royal Marines and Police Firearms Officers past and present, whom I had the enormous pleasure of calling my colleagues.

Acknowledgements

This book would not have been possible without the help and support of Sarah, my wife. I would also like to thank Debbie W., Chris F., and Reuben for their encouragement and ideas.

CHAPTER ONE

Pure evil, he often wondered whether it was something that a person was born with, or did it grow, fester, and develop inside a man until it could no longer be contained? Thirty years' combined service serving his country had not given him the definitive answer but now, as he increased the pressure on his trigger finger staring down the Glock with both eyes open into Thomas Burns's chest, he saw it all clearly and he knew for certain that he had his answer. The eyes told him everything; they held no fear, just hatred and rage. It was as he had always suspected: the evil had always been there Reuben had seen it before, not often but had seen it. When Thomas Burns's mother had given birth, she would have seen it if she had looked closely enough, but instead she had ignored the signs, pulled her child to her breast, and nourished him. It would have been far better, Reuben thought, to have strangled the child at birth and saved the couple that lay dead inside the house from such a violent death. Now the choice was his. Just a little more pressure and he would send the first of two rounds into the centre of the mass, which stood so defiantly in front of him. The rounds would leave the chamber, almost as one, the individual shots merging into one hitting the chest with the force of a mule kick and, once and for all, eradicate the evil. Burns glared back at him.

"You don't have the guts to pull the trigger," he snarled.

Reuben and his team were Eelite Police Firearms Officers, specialists in hostage rescue, formed in response to a world that was changing, a world where armed criminals and terrorists were becoming commonplace. He had been there from day one; he was the first to raise his hand and volunteer when the unit was conceived and one of the first eight to attend the specialist training course at Devon and Cornwall's Police Firearms Range. He arrived for evaluation and left as a new member of a new elite tactical response force. The instructors knew that he had the skills and the desire to succeed but as soon as the training began, they realised that he also easily gained the respect of those around him. His successful progression into the new unit was never in doubt. The Force had a coastline of over 500 miles which offered ideal training conditions for the Royal Marine Commando Units which included the Commando Training Centre at Lympstone and 42 Commando which was based just outside of Plymouth. This provided the police recruiters with a high number of potentially exceptional police officers who would already be disciplined and efficient; their knowledge of firearms was an added skill that the Force could use.

Thirteen eventful years as a Royal Marine followed by ten in the police force had taught him all he needed to know. He had taken the knowledge and refined it. Now after a busy and hectic stint on the armed response vehicles and countless operations with firearms, he had become invaluable. He would use his skills to hunt down and arrest this new, more dangerous breed of criminal that threatened the peaceful existence of the people he had sworn to protect.

If Reuben had a fault it was this, he hated these criminals who committed their despicable acts and then used the judicial process to escape justice. He detested the weak judges and corrupt lawyers who took the criminals and turned them into innocent victims of circumstance. He despaired as social workers stood in front of the court and explained that exceptional circumstances meant that the defendants were not responsible for their actions.

The Burns twins were wrong: Reuben did have the guts; he could have pulled the trigger and then gone for pizza with his crew, and he would have slept peacefully without nightmares and never given them a second thought again; it would have been easy. He eased his finger from the trigger and lowered his gun. Burns smirked.

"Told you, pig, you are gutless."

As Reuben's colleagues shackled the stocky 6' 4" prisoner he holstered his Glock 17 Pistol with chambered round. He ensured his thumb closed over the weapon pushing the safety strap into place. His eyes were locked on the body in front of him, his hand rested on his thigh holster as his colleagues loaded the prisoner into the waiting Range Rover.

Burns was handcuffed and placed in the rear of the vehicle. The escorting officer checked the restraints and made his way around the vehicle. Reuben took hold of the open door and started to close it. As the gap between the door and the pillar narrowed, he leant in close to the prisoner; the smell of stale cigarettes and cheap body spray seeped into his nostrils. Burns turned to his left and made eye contact with him. A tooth-stained grin appeared on his pockmarked face.

"What the fuck are you looking at, filth," he spat. Reuben hesitated, his eyes were colder and harsher than Burns's; they locked onto his prisoner's and did not blink.

"One day, my friend, one day," he murmured.

The puzzled expression on the prisoner's face turned into a frown.

"You're talking shit pal, what the shit does that mean? What about one day—what the fuck are you talking about, you pig?" Reuben pulled his head back slightly and glanced at the other officers busily preparing for the journey.

He leant even closer. "We will meet again, maybe not for a while, maybe not for years, but we will, and when we do, I will be ready for you, so look at my face… remember it."

Burns laughed but there was no humour in his eyes.

"You'd better be Quick Draw McGraw then, plod, because if I see you first you won't live long."

Reuben pulled his head out of the car, straightened up, closed the door, and tapped the roof of the car. Burns settled back into the seat with a grin on his face; the yellow tobacco-stained teeth were the last thing that Reuben saw. The car screeched off as the driver turned the lights and sirens on and began its journey back to base.

Killer and police officer would meet again and only one of them would survive the encounter.

CHAPTER TWO

November 5th, 2004

Reuben's team comprised eight men, two vehicles and a multitude of munitions. Each man was a volunteer and had to have passed a rigorous selection. During the selection and subsequent courses, they were looked at closely to place each man into a specific role. From the outset, it was clear that his build and tenacity, suited the role of MOE (Method of Entry). If you needed a sniper, an explosives expert or negotiator you called on this team, call sign Foxtrot One. They were a tight-knit group. They trained hard and fought harder, each man had complete faith in the man who stood next to him. The police had spent thousands on training, both in Force and at countless venues around the country, including the Special Boat Service, Killing House in Pool, Dorset.

These teams were a fearless, highly trained 'can do' bunch of adrenalin junkies.

It was November the fifth, 2004, Bonfire night and always one of the busiest nights of the year; the public always found it difficult to tell the difference between a gunshot and a firework. The team were expecting plenty of calls tonight; most of the calls would be a waste of time and effort but each would be treated the same and each report would fully have investigated. The shift began at 1500 hours, and they were a punctual group; if one of their numbers had not arrived by 1445 hours the others would begin searching for him. As usual Reuben was first on station. He turned his 1992 Honda Fire Blade sports motorcycle into the car park, the aftermarket exhaust can announcing his arrival to the neighbourhood a minute or so earlier. He had left his house an hour earlier, to storm around the sweeping B roads of Devon before his shift began. He gave a final twist on the throttle, deafening Colin the civilian car cleaner who was nearby and smiling in delight as the engine roared in response. He strode across the tarmacked car park, past the impeccably parked liveried police patrol cars. The team shared the Traffic Centre within the Headquarters and he looked at the row of Volvos and Range Rovers. Being a traffic officer was a prerequisite of being a member of the team, as you had to have been an advanced driver. The thought of screwing a driver for an obscured number plate, and issuing a thirty-pound ticket, did not hold any excitement whatsoever.

He entered the code into the rigid heavy door and pulled it open. A quick glance around the office confirmed that he was alone. He headed into the locker room, took off his bike leathers and hung them neatly on the rack alongside his uniform He pulled out a spotlessly clean plain black T-shirt, pulled it over his head and threaded his huge legs into a pair of pristine black trousers. He pulled them up to his waist, tightened the belt, grabbed his baseball cap from its hook and placed it on his head. He stared at the figure in the mirror and winced as he realised that the hair was thinner these days and the lines across his brow were becoming more pronounced. However, despite the signs of ageing, he was happy, the muscular frame and rock-hard biceps were still things to be proud of; he was confident that he had more than enough to convince the most hardened criminal that he was prepared to mix it with the best, as dirty as you like. He patted his stomach, sucked it in a little and made a mental note to ease up on the late-night crap. He moved back into the office and headed into the kitchen, filling the kettle with freezing water and flicked the power switch down. If the drinks were not ready for the team, they would be complaining all night. Rick and Brian opened the door and came in. They had come straight from the gym so their hair was wet and their faces were red. Both had showered and already donned their T-shirts and trousers. They were ready for the shift or at least they would be when their drinks were placed in front of them. The heavy plodding sound from outside indicated that Jason had arrived. He plugged in his code and pushed the door open.

Reuben gave him a disapproving scowl. "You look like something the fuckin cat dragged in; get yourself cleaned up before Phil gets here."

Jason replied by smiling and raising his middle finger. "Twat," Reuben said, they chuckled as Jason headed off for a shower. Mick, Simon and Tim came in together. All with a sheepish look on their face. Reuben figured it had been a long night that involved lots of drinking and array of tall stories. By 1500 hours, everyone was on station except the gaffer Phil who was in a meeting. By 1510 hours, they had all been served with a steaming hot mug of tea courtesy of second in command Reuben and they were ready for the night ahead. Each man had slipped seamlessly into his role. As a unit, there was nothing that could faze them, they were trained to deal with anything they would encounter over the next twelve hours, but they were not to know that this shift would push them to their limits and would last more than twenty-four hours. They would start with a dead body in Plymouth and end up vowing to find the maniacs who fired shotguns into the heads of a Cornish mother and young daughter.

Phil breezed in, called them to the table and began chatting informally across the table, shifting his gaze from man to man. He settled on Reuben and noted the imperceptible nod that told him he was satisfied that everyone was ready for duty. Despite their friendly banter of the earlier thirty minutes Reuben had spent the time scrutinising each of them as they chatted and sipped at their tea. He had searched for faults and found none.

The Force had put together two teams, Foxtrot One, based in Exeter, and Foxtrot Two, based in Plympton near Plymouth.

In the years preceding the formation of the teams, Devon and Cornwall had recruited heavily from the localities which including the Army, Naval, and Royal Marine bases, such as the Commando Training Centre. These locations had a ready supply of mature, fit and experienced people, ideal for recruitment into the police service, at a time when funding was plentiful, and ideas were flying around.

Such an idea was Armed Response Vehicles/Crews and Specialist Firearms teams.

It was decided that the Firearms Officers would be recruited from officers who had a Police Advanced Driver Authorisation, because of the need to crew high-performance vehicles. At the time recruitment was from existing traffic officers, who were already authorised. This included all of Foxtrot One's team bar one, and this was almost the same as Foxtrot Two's team. The specialist teams were still on the drawing board initially.

Despite this Force being mainly a rural Force, it also had a number a large city and town areas, such as Exeter, Plymouth, Torquay, and Truro. Initially, work was slow; however, as the crews became more familiar with their surroundings an intelligence was provided to them, they soon became remarkably busy. Drugs were being brought into the counties from elsewhere and as such, brought with them the criminal fraternity that were used to dealing drugs in places such as London, Liverpool, Manchester, and Bristol.

With these criminal groups came individuals who were used to carrying knives and/or guns which ensured that the armed response vehicles were kept busy for all their shifts

Initially, armed response vehicles worked from three areas, being Exeter, Plymouth, and Bodmin in North Devon. At any one time in Devon and Cornwall there were three double-crewed units available, and this would ensure that a minimum of six people could attend any incident in any time.

It was decided earlier on that the vehicles to be used would have to be fast enough and big enough to do your job effectively. Cars such as Vauxhall Omegas, Volvos and Range Rovers were used.

It quickly became clear that the best all-round vehicle was the manual Range Rover.

The crews were able to work within their own time limits wherever they wanted unless they were given a specific task. Each vehicle was answerable to the control command centre and duty officer equally and they had phones linked to each of the vehicles. The dress code for the officers was the same as any other police officer and included rudimentary body armour. As their successes became well known within the police, there was no shortage of people wanting to do it, and selection and training was frequent and at an extremely high level.

The requirements were specific, although ex-military had an advantage. Prospective officers came from a variety of backgrounds. Recruitment was by way of a paper shift and interview process and obviously a firearms test on the range.

Many fell by the wayside at the range because of the use of pistols, which are not an easy weapon to use effectively. Once on the team you could expect a busy, varied and often stressful shift, dealing with the worst and seeing the worst society can present to us.

Within Foxtrot One, all the individuals brought to the table, a vast amount of skill. As luck would have it the majority, were ex-Royal Marines and as such thought alike. The team ethos and work ethic were to be the best; training was regular, hard, and physically demanding.

Overtime, quite rightly, was always available, and the armed response crews became an elite, and were envied not only in Devon and Cornwall but by other forces around the country. This was shown many times in cross force training where Devon and Cornwall officers attended other centres around the country and competed in and trained with other groups and other forces. Devon and Cornwall were always triumphant. Their budget was so extensive that equipment clothing and vehicles wanted for nothing. Initially it was estimated that each officer had been issued approximately three thousand pounds worth of extra kit, excluding weapons and munitions, in the early days of implementation.

The nature of the role attracts persons who had active pastimes or interests. Things such as motorcycling, shooting, surfing, triathlons and the like; in short, adrenalin junkies.

When training, all the three areas would train together as part of the same team so despite being or working from different geographical areas you knew the individuals well and everybody got on well.

Phil spent a few minutes bringing them up to speed on the day's events and the latest developments on their earlier cases: a couple of well-known characters arrested for possession of Class A drugs in Exeter, they would be off the streets for a day or two before the circus of lawyers, judges, and bail hearings began. A death just outside Crediton that seemed suspicious at first but now looked like natural causes. An old boy who had walked in off the street with a sawn-off shotgun in a duffle bag and an idiot who had spent four hours threatening to jump off a bridge near junction 30 of the M5. All standard fare, nothing that needed their immediate attention. He moved on to the shift that lay ahead. There was trouble in Plymouth, something to do with a naval rating and a gun he said, but that was all he knew for now. He shrugged and gestured towards his phone.

"Still waiting for an update from the control room, shouldn't be long now. I expect we will be on our way pretty soon." They groaned in unison, Reuben swore under his breath and grimaced: Plymouth, the docks, Bonfire night, not a good mix especially if a gun was involved. Jason rubbed his hands together, a nervous habit that he had when the adrenalin began to flow, his face lit up when Plymouth was mentioned.

"I fuckin' love Plymouth," he muttered. Jason had spent a time in Plymouth and its dockyards as a young midshipman. His time there had opened his eyes to the delights of dockyards and all the frivolous people and incidents they seem to attract. A couple of them shook their heads in mock disgust. Reuben, Simon and Phil had all been Royal Marines; although they had served in different units, all of them had spent a portion of their time in Plymouth and they understood exactly what Jason was on about.

"Fucking Plymouth indeed; we all know what you love about it you perverted fucker," said Simon as his mind flicked backed to Diamond Lolls in Union Street *Happy days,* he thought. *Happy days.* Phil ignored the comments; Reuben tapped his finger against his temple to show that his mate was crazy. Phil fished around in his drawer and pulled out a handful of A5 photographs which he spread out on the table and motioned towards them. This was a regular and ever-changing ritual of pinging people's faces, fixing them in their minds with one short glance, a visual check of this week's mugshots, a collection of the divisions most wanted criminals. Maybe a few faces who had escaped arrest or justice. Then there were the nasty bastards and the nutcases. Once seen, never forgotten; the team took each face and placed it in their memory banks. It is amazing how the brain digests images and then trawls them up out of the depths and matches a face on the street with a photo they had seen weeks or months earlier. The team had made several unexpected arrests in the past on the strength of a single full-face photo, the most memorable being the day Reuben and Brian called in for a pasty in Launceston and came out of the shop with two of Devon's most sought-after criminals.

Before Phil could utter another word, his mobile rang, he grabbed it from the table and pressed receive.

"Control Room, Inspector Mr Cannes on the line," he said. After a few nods and couple of curt questions, he ended the call and stuffed the phone into his front pocket. "Job's on boys, get your shit together, we are off to Plymouth, firearms incident—full kit. I'll get updates on the way and keep you informed."

Each man slipped into the routine easily; the training kicked in and it all happened naturally. They moved into the locker room and began to collect their kit. Reuben pulled out his body armour and pulled at the Taser to check that it was secure. Next, he grabbed his kit complete with ballistic helmet, total balaclava and iridium ski goggles. The kit was completed by a set of wraparound ear defenders; he removed them from the bag and slung them around his neck.

Each man received a radio along with a spare battery. Reuben opened his laptop, logged on and updated their status to active, everyone else that logged on within Devon and Cornwall Police would now know that they were on the road. If their status changed, they could update it from their radios as they drove towards Plymouth; even a simple coffee break could be logged and recorded. The way this was done was by using what is known as the 'ten codes'. Quite simply it makes radio communication, more importantly, statuses, universal, without a lot of unnecessary chit-chat.

Led by Phil they moved out of the office and down the steps into the car park. Reuben pulled the door closed and pushed his shoulder against it to check that it was secure. He took the steps three at a time and caught up with the team at the door armoury, Phil plugged in his code, and they moved inside to collect and sign for their weapons.

Each took his usual weapons: Reuben started with the 9mm Glock 17 self-loading pistol. He added two magazines which gave him twenty rounds. Next, he took a Heckler and Koch MP5 submachine gun from the shelf and added two full magazines of 20 x 9 mm rounds. As a backup, he chose his favourite weapon in the room, a cut down Remington shotgun and his thigh strap with twenty assorted cartridges. *More than enough for one Bonfire night,* he thought.

Each scribbled their names, checked, and double-checked against the list. They each took their two kit bags that held their two stones in weight of kit; the first held firearms equipment and the second contained their riot gear. They were fully loaded and as ready as they would ever be. Phil shouted to them all to load up the vehicles and prepare to leave; the men did not need to be told their roles, but he issued the order anyway. He stood in the middle of the car park with his mobile close to his ear as the latest update was coming through from the control room. He finished the call and pointed towards Mick.

"You drive the Range Rover and Brian takes the Sprinter, with Reuben as my wingman."

The men nodded and clambered into the driver's seats; the other four split up. They were evenly balanced: four men in each vehicle.

Although everyone knew that the four wheel drive car would get to any incident first, hence putting the four within into any incident first, there was no jealousy, or throwing of teddies into the corners. It was always a case of 'swings and roundabouts', as nobody knew whether this job, or the next one would be the job that stretched everyone's skills sets to the max, or would involve shots being fired, either from the police, or God forbid a suspect's weapon. Most scenarios dictated that the teams would have to await the arrival of the van in any case, due to the kit it carried, or requirement for a second four-man team.

Phil's mobile rang again; this was turning into the real thing. They pulled out of the Police Headquarters at Middlemoor Exeter. It was situated for its easy access to both either the M5, A38 or North Devon link road. On this occasion, they were to join the M5 Southbound, which would link into the A38. Traffic was thankfully light, aided by the activation of blue lights and sirens. Within minutes, both vehicles had joined the M5 at Junction 30 taking the third exit signposted to A38 A380. It was minutes again until they reached the junction for the A38 Plymouth bound. From here they had a straightforward high-speed route directly into Plymouth; even at a conservative 120 mph they would be there in less than twenty minutes, conscious they would have to fill the thirsty Range Rover shortly after arrival (half a tank at best at 120mph plus). Pete updated them all at the same time via the radio. They were receiving what is known as 'hot info', it was fluid, rapid, and often needed confirmation, collaboration, or repetition. One overwhelming fact was repeatedly coming through the different avenues of communication: they believed the individual to be armed. The three armed response vehicles which were also Range Rovers, but in full police spec had been dispatched. The double crews were all handpicked, and most had a military background. The selection and later firearms courses were not as easy as some thought. Pistol skills were often the downfall of some of the applicants, even more so the demanding and intensive Police Advanced Driving courses. Although initially to function as a containment, at any incident where the suspect is (armed or otherwise so violent that he/she can only be safely restrained without the use of firearms) is thought to be armed, they could also enter and search if the situation dictated.

CHAPTER THREE

Phil confirmed with the Control Room that the area was secure, and no further action would be taken until they arrived to take over. With the assistance of the family and negotiators at the scene, he expected the job to be over either before they got there, or at the very worst, an early entry to locate and disarm the rating. His mind momentarily drifted off to an old wartime black-and-white film he had seen many times, where the stars, upon hearing of their undoubtedly suicidal mission, had laughed it off with a flyaway comment such as "We will be home in time for tea and biscuits, chaps!"

The Range Rover approached the roundabout at a speed which could have done with being about 20mph slower, the two-ton behemoth stuck well to the road forcing the occupants against the windows, and bringing Phil back to the task in hand. He looked disapprovingly at the driver.

"When is your Advanced refresher you knob, for fuck's sake?"

On arrival at the RV, they would receive a full briefing and formulate a plan, so no further instructions were necessary. He slipped the radio back into its pouch and caught sight of Jason's grinning face in his rear-view mirror.

Fucking nutcase, he thought. *But I'm glad he's with us and not against us.*

The vehicles travelled together, overtaking everything that lay in front of them, a rep in his Company's Vauxhall, who was doodling at his steady 80mph in lane two, would be brought back to the here and now by the blazing headlights and blue strobes which were closing the distance at an incredible speed behind him. The drivers swung off at Marsh Mills and killed all the noise. Jason pointed through to the front passenger area, and onwards to the first of three speed cameras, as the Range Rover belted through. Looking in the rear-facing mirror, Phil saw Jason's face silhouetted by the noticeable double flash of the revenue collector. He hated them and spoke into his radio.

"Echo Victor from Foxtrot One, we have buzzed the first set of lights on the embankment."

The reply was swift. "Roger, please confirm your registration." As he passed the information, they hit the second lot. The operator back in Exeter did not require the notification and noted it on the log that he was updating. Experience had proved that the high banks and natural direction of the estuary would carry the noise of the convoy all the way down towards their destination. Phil contacted the inspector on the radio and told him they were on blues but would make a silent approach as the veered left towards the docks. They eased off the gas and slipped quickly through the streets. When the lights showed red, they ignored them and sped across when it was safe to do so, they were confident that the situation at the scene was under control but the sooner they arrived the sooner they could deal with the incident. The streets were already busy with children and parents heading for bonfires and displays. Radio chatter had slowed down now and the rapid flow of information from all angles had slowed to a trickle, it was mostly logistical information, and the odd request about toilet breaks and provision for refreshments. There had been no further operational updates since they arrived on the outskirts of the city. The van had made brilliant progress, and, incredibly, was behind the car, Phil had seen the big Mercedes van getting close, as they had come off Marsh Mills, and gave himself a little smile as they began to skirt around the dockyard, following the fence with its barbed wire top and moving CCTV cameras that discouraged unauthorised access. Mick turned right and then took a sharp left along Balfour Terrace, avoiding with care the rows of vehicles parked both sides and then took the right fork into Garden Street. They saw their first officers, two on the right-hand pavement and two on the left, all four of them placed in the vicinity to spread calm and reassure the public. Healy Terrace lay on their left; they swung in past another a group of uniformed bobbies and drove up to the cordon. Phil's vehicle pulled up and Brian pulled in behind them in the thrashed Sprinter. From now they were subject to a different chain of command. Incident Commander Superintendent Harry Pears would now be giving them their instructions via Phil.

Reuben jumped out of the Sprinter and surveyed the scene noting the mobile command centre housed inside another silver long wheelbase Mercedes Sprinter. Here they would kit up, grab some food, and prepare for the operation. Officers everywhere, two armed response vehicles each with its own crew and a shedload of Devon and Cornwall's constables. He spat on the floor and grunted in disgust—all these resources for one stupid youth who could easily be fast asleep in the house at the end of the road. It drove him crazy; his team were the best in the country, they were well prepared, and their powerful armoury was second to none, but it was wasted on operations like this. The job was not always exciting; he accepted that as part of the job. Not every call they received could mean action; often the patrols were laborious and dull. Highlights of the night could often be a group of youths throwing eggs or a youngster dropping a firework through a terrified neighbour's letterbox. The elderly and defenceless were ideal targets for the modern-day youths. The whole team had seen it all before. Quite often their job was a waste of labour and time; the destinations were painfully familiar, and the faces were often the same. The reward for this behaviour was often not the cell time that you might expect, instead the offenders would be whisked off to paintballing days or go carting sessions at the local track, and the taxpayer would foot the bill later. These days 'off' were organised by the local Neighbourhood Officer in tandem with other agencies. They were designed to distract the youngsters from taking part in such antics.

Despite all of this, when the engines fired, and the vehicles left their base, each man tensed their muscles and focused on the job ahead. Secretly each kept the same thought circulating in their heads… this could be the big one and you had to be ready for it. He turned this thought over in his head. It felt like a tumble dryer, going around and round, stopping starting. The updating of information increased the load, but there was one thought that always pushed its way to the front, the nagging almost annoying one. If it came to it, if it came to ending someone's life, could he do it? It was a big ask, something which he had come close to doing in the Royal Marines, but that was different, much, much different. The 'enemy' then was exactly that, the enemy. Here in overcast Devon, there were different things to take on board, *Rules Of Engagement*. He swore under his breath. *Fucking rules.*

Mick broke his train of thought and pushed him towards the gazebo.

"Come on old man, you are in a world of your own there. Grab your gear and let us get inside and sort this mess out.' Phil moved off towards the command centre.

"Briefing in ten!" he said over his shoulder. "Get yourselves kitted out then sort some scran and wets—it might be the last you will get for a while." (Scran and wets were Royal Marines' jargon for food and drink.) They strode towards the tent; local bobbies cast envious glances at them and nodded nervous greetings. The team ignored them, not because they were above them or that their shit did not smell, it was simply because they were not a factor in what was about to happen, a small cog in a huge fucking clock. A seasoned female traffic officer stopped the team at the door to the sterile area, she was dressed in head to toe in high-vis gear and had wrapped a thick woollen scarf around her neck. Most of the team knew Sarah, a married officer based at Plymouth now, from their stints on traffic before the Firearms world lured them away. Annual driving refreshers maintained contact with most of the Traffic Department throughout Devon and Cornwall. There was a little of 'them and us', which had started with the older drivers, most of whom had retired by now. They had neutered this feeling, and often made it clear, believing the driving standards had dropped. The normal traffic officers were known as black rats and had bought anonymous little black rats to stick on their own personal cars, almost like the Christian fish symbols one can see on many cars.

Sarah wrote down each name and ushered them inside, the temperature was already dropping, and it was going to be a long frosty night unless the boy with the gun decided to come quietly. A voice was droning on in the background, some distance away. The team hesitated to make out what was being said and by whom.

"Reminds me of the old war films where translators are trying to persuade the enemy to give up, never worked then either

," said John, with a wry grin, which prompted a tirade of abuse, which was squared away by Phil.

"Knock it on the fucking head, you."

It was negotiators attempting to get the lad to make contact and enter into some sort of dialogue. The relentless droning suggested that it was not working, and that they were desperate to make contact. Someone was trying to talk the youth out of the house; they did not fancy their chances. If the youth had not responded in the last hour, he was unlikely to reply now. Reuben dropped his kit bags on the floor and winced as the trapped nerve in his shoulder sent a sharp reminder. *Fucking hell,* he thought. Mick had suggested it may be sciatica, but Reuben knew it was too many nights spent in cold damp holes and thick wet undergrowth often for hours at a time. Soon it would be time to leave this all to the youngsters, retire and get a nice little comfortable driving job to supplement his pension. He thought of the wife and how she liked to spend money and decided he might have to continue for another year or two. He did not mind his family having the pleasant things in life. Sarah, his lovely patient wife, had often been left at an opportune moment because of a pager going off, left to get a taxi home, or make last arrangements. They had all spoken about the abstractions and life at the end of a pager many times. She had been with Reuben long enough to remember the relentless training and often extended absences whilst training, often going to bed at night without him and waking after he had left early the following morning. Never asking where or why unless he offered to share the earlier shift's activities. To be fair it was often boring, for her anyway. Sarah knew that there would always be a nice foreign break somewhere warm during the following year.

The team were all busy unpacking their gear and starting to

get kitted up, body armour on, communications fired up, assessed, and activated. Rick started first, when he noticed everyone was miked up.

"Hello, all call signs, this is Rick. Radio test call, over."

The replies filtered in

"Rick from Reuben strength 5 over."

"Phil ok's over."

After the radios had been checked, Mick moved away over to the radio box in the Sprinter mumbling as he went.

"What's up mate?" Phil shouted.

Mick fumbled in the box, with his right hand whilst throwing his throat mike to the ground on top of his kit bag.

"Load of English shit, why couldn't we get the Jap stuff we trialled?"

"How is it that its always yours? Everyone else's is fine, and never lets us down," Jason called across and held up a small black pouch. "Stop fucking dripping; you can borrow my spare ones but they've got my name on so don't think about half inching them you pikey twat."

He tossed them over, and Rick caught them mid-flight. He turned to Mick who was red in the face and had his arm extended catching air.

"You're slowing big man." He passed them over to Mick as he could see it was not a suitable time or place to wind the big gym monster up. He snatched them, held Rick's eye contact and muttered, "Wanker."

CHAPTER FOUR

In the background, the voice on the loudhailer drifted across towards them. The traffic all around was becoming scarce. They guessed that there had still been no reply from inside the house and figured that it would be down to them to find the young naval rating.

Phil pushed his way into the tent and then turned and pulled down the zip, ensuring there were no little ears listening to give them some privacy. He was admired by all of them but was famously short-tempered due to a nagging back pain and an equally painful ex-wife who rarely left him in peace. He rubbed the small of his back with his hand and massaged his upper hip with his thumb and forefinger. Reuben called the men together and they grouped around their boss in anticipation of an update on the situation. He gestured to remove their helmets and ear defenders, which were also their communications setups. He was clearly agitated but as always, he came straight to the point; the men knew that they could ask questions later, for now they huddled up and gave him their full attention.

"OK boys, we have a young rating, Christopher Nobbs, aged 21, born and bred in Plymouth. No earlier record other than the odd run-in with the police in his early teens. He was called into see his superiors this morning on a disciplinary matter. Seems he did not take to well to being told off and he stormed out of the meeting and issued some threats about getting a gun and shooting someone.

"Boss has confirmed that he is not a firearms licence holder, and that this is out of character. This is also confirmed by the MOD. His Chief Petty Officer told us that the incident for which he was to be spoken about is a storm in a teacup, but Nobbs has got wound up about it He had repeated the threats when he returned to his quarters and then left the building. Approximately an hour later he is seen by one of his friends on the road adjacent to this one. The witness reports that he was carrying a long-barrelled rifle which we are assuming was a high velocity weapon. The area was secured two hours ago, and there has been no sign of activity inside the building. His father has arrived and has spent the last hour calling him on the loudhailer but there has been no response. The situation is fluid, but I don't think he's coming out so let's assume we're going to have to go in and find him." Phil paused for a second to allow the information to sink in. "Plymouth boys have an ETA of seven minutes; once they are here and kitted up we will move to our positions. Teams are the same as always, me Simon, Rick and Brian, Reuben, Mick and Jason and Tim. Plymouth boys will pair off when they arrive, from now on we're Alpha and Plymouth are Bravo." He held up a folder and waved it at them. "The council have forwarded a floor plan of the building—make sure you commit it to memory before you take up your positions."

He dropped the folder on the makeshift table, swung around and grabbed his own kit bags which Brian had got from the van, and dropped them into the only bit of free space he could find, Reuben looked up, nodded and continued to get his kit squared away. Each man settled into his routine and prepared himself mentally for the coming hours. Whenever they debriefed, the subject of what was going through each other's mind on any op would always pop up, it was almost a comfort blanket for some of them. Reuben always went back to his Royal Marine days. He was not Corps pissed, the term used by ex-Boot necks like himself, for people that cannot let the Service go after leaving. It was more putting all the challenging work, and extreme training to effective use. *If I could do all that,* he thought, *everything else is a walk in the park.*

Once their preparations were complete, they would have four groups each comprising four men. Alpha group would supply two men and Bravo group the other two. Multi-agency work would try to obtain floor plans as a matter of urgency. Sometimes it was easier to do than other occasions, depending on factors, often beyond anyone's control. The two biggest obstacles to getting these important pieces of information were weather and date/time, not always in that order. In any case someone would have obtained a visual of any location, and where a building is involved, colour coordinated it, for ease of descriptions when relaying instructions or using comms.

Quite simply the building, or indeed plane or vessel, would be split into colours and levels.

As one would look at what is the agreed front of anything, it would be white; the rear, black; the left, red and the right, green, funnily enough the same as port and starboard on planes and vessels at sea. Each level would be numbered, so ground floor or lowest level would be level one, next level two, etc. Every aperture from left to right would also be numbered. A good example of this is a front first-floor bedroom window which would be, *white two one*.

Each group would assume their designated position to ensure that the entire house was covered and secure. Reuben and his group were assigned the rear of the house (Black).

'Black', the rear of the house, had three windows and a door on level one which became Black 1/1 Black 1/2, Black 1/3 and Black 1/4. Reuben's responsibility was to continually scan all the apertures. The first job for each man was to sketch their designated building view, and for any interesting features they would take a notepad and sketch everything they saw. He noted that the door was a heavy one. Squinting through his Heckler and Koch MP5 red dot sight, he saw that it was a solid old Victorian type of door.

Bollocks, he thought. *If we must go in on this face, through that door we will have to use many door opening options. These are available and close to hand in the Sprinter.*

Reuben discussed this with Brian who was busy sketching what they were discussing. He looked up and said, "Hey mate, have a butcher through these," and passed over a small pair of mint Gerber binoculars, petite but with an amazing zoom. As good as they were, it did not reveal anything to help his decision.

"Brian, it's a shit job. If we must enter through that door, we'll be smacking it for hours if it isn't open; we'd have to get authority to shotgun it."

Brian accepted the bins as Reuben passed them back, and a wry smile widened on Brian's face. Reuben had the Remington Wing Master Shotgun slung under his arm on a bungee cord.

"Have you got Hatton rounds mate?" Although he had, he subconsciously fingered the thigh wallet he wore with the assortment of shotgun rounds. Years of being a shotgunner and method of entry officer had impregnated his muscle memory with the location of each round. There was an assortment of varied sizes of bird shot, and Hatten rounds. The Hatten round, a lethal solid lump of lead in a cartridge, was used for locks hinges, and dispatching of large animals such as bulls, cows and suchlike. If an entry through the door was going to go ahead, he would have to empty the five rounds of medium shot and replace it with the Hatten. Even though the rounds were for destroying the door upon entry, in times of immediacy they could be used against a suspect, negating the need to unload and replace. During training, Reuben had seen images of an armed suspect killed by the police in the early eighties, using a shotgun with similar rounds. If needed it would stop at once with devastating results any determined and armed suspect. It did not take long for Brian to finish the sketch. He looked at it.

"I'm not no Rembrandt," Brian mumbled.

"Indeed, Brian, indeed; in fact, it is simply shit, but it will do," and laughed.

Once all positions had completed their sketches Jason crawled around everyone collected them, passed over a plastic bottle of water, lukewarm Cornish pasty and took them back to the incident commander who would add the information to the system. A line in the sand was always drawn and agreed with each member of the group; where possible they would always avoid the use of lethal force but if the target crossed this line, the group would use their weapons to ensure he or she came no further.

A Baton gun had been taken by each team of two, with two spare baton rounds. The line in the sand would also be the point at which the baton gun is either discharged or not, negating the need for any discussion.

At about 2225hrs, all the teams were in position. The house was dark and silent; there was no movement inside. Fireworks lit the sky with annoying regularity and lit up the house as they exploded, and even though the bangs were expected, the men still found it difficult not to flinch as the sound echoed off the walls of the old Victorian house. Four of the Bravo Team had crept around the rear, scaled a small stone wall, and then crept to within ten metres of 'Black'—the rear of the house. They were lying silently on the stone chippings that were used as a barbeque area in the warmer summer months. One pair, George and Mark, stretched out to their right; all four of them were watching the house intently. The four men had agreed on their line in the sand, it extended from a plant pot on the right of the patio, ran across their front and terminated at the trunk of an old crab apple tree to their left. If the lad came out of the rear, they would do all they could to convince him to give himself up but if he crossed this line, and he had a weapon, they would shoot him. All sixteen men were linked by a highly efficient communications system; each had a throat mike and earpiece, so transmitting was as easy as depressing the thumb switch and relaying your message. As midnight approached, the fireworks grew more frenetic; rockets sped across the sky and filled the night with their colourful patterns. As soon as the new day began, the crescendo diminished as the revellers finished their last few drinks and headed home. Communication from every team had been silent for fifteen minutes but now the reports began again.

One by one each group reported in.

"White no change." The men at the front were confirming that their section was quiet.

"Red no change." Nothing happening to the left of the building.

"Green no change."

Reuben clicked with his thumb and reported, "Black no change, no movement in the house." He released the pressure on the activator and winked at Brian. "Little fucker is either fast asleep or dead I reckon; about time the commander ordered us in I'd say. A dog would be good if they can find one, might save us a lot of time." Brian nodded in agreement but didn't utter a sound, all of them would have preferred to stand up and get themselves into the house but the order had not been given, for now they were stuck amongst the pebbles of the makeshift patio.

The hours ticked by slowly with the silence interrupted by short, sharp updates from each side of the house, but the story was still the same: they saw no one and heard no one. Even the moon had started to retire for the night; it was pitch-black and the temperature had dropped below freezing point, pockets of frost were forming in the garden and attaching themselves to the pathetic blades of grass that grew there. As the night wore on, the ground in front of them turned white and glistened whenever the moon popped its head through the dense cloud. It would be dawn soon; still no sign of life inside the house. The order would come soon, they were all expecting it; they could not stay here forever. In the distance, they heard a dog barking, and smiled.

"Won't be long now," he murmured to no one.

Phil's voice came across the airwaves; it was crystal clear to the point that he could have been standing right next to them.

"The search dog is here; we have permission to enter and locate. Stand by."

All sixteen men had supported their positions for almost eight hours; they were tired, hungry, and cold but the news that they had received permission to enter sent the blood coursing through their veins. They all slowly stood up, still at a crouch, everyone being covered with a weapon by their respective partners who were scanning their areas of concern keeping both eyes open.

Brian stifled a groan, as he rose.

"Old twat," he said.

Reuben remained in the crouch as he rose, its catching he

thought as his knees cracked, sounding like the clackers American Airborne allied troops used on D-Day, to communicate with friendly forces.

No movement without covering fire, the first rules of moving with weapons in a hostile environment. This engrained rule was clear as each team watched each other move to the Lay Up Point for a pre-entry brief.

The radio whispered, "Black moves up to the door."

Reuben and Brian were the last team to link up with the others which included Phil and Simon the other teams sergeant.

Beside Phil was Doug the dog handler with Buzz, his German Alsatian. Buzz was lying quietly, and seemingly disinterested in his role. Doug had fitted a video and harness to Buzz and had passed the mobile monitor to one of the other team members, Jim, who would be number one on the entry team. Looking over at the image displayed, relayed from the camera on Buzz's head, to be fair the clarity was amazing.

Phil's voice interrupted the silence.

"All teams move forward. Bravos one and two will enter along with the dog. Jim will have the screen relaying from the dog."

The teams edged closer to the house until their backs were against the side wall, hidden from view, off the shingled drive. Jim turned on the monitor. The screen was blank but soon lit up displaying the grass that Buzz had buried his head into. He giggled to himself and showed the screen to Simon his number two. Simon smiled and nodded; it would show the progress of the dog and hopefully the young man within.

Bravo's team leader led his team to the side door, on Green which was a porch door and appeared to be open.

They set up on the door, years of practice negated any

speech. As Jim reached the door, he felt a squeeze on his shoulder which was a signal passed forward by each man from the rear to say all were in place. Without a word, they waited, MP5 in hand as Mike the entry man slid in front ready to gain entry.

Jim heard heavy panting to his right it was Buzz and Doug, quiet as you like, he thought. Glancing down at the screen he could see Mike's arse as he reached to the door, followed by Buzz sniffing. Mike found the door to be closed but unlocked. He gently eased the door open and moved back into his position as the number three letting the dog and Doug take the lead. Jim followed at once behind almost as a congenital twin, his hand on the shoulder of dog handler, to let him know he had his back covered, and to control the progress. Buzz was on a loose lead controlled by Doug. The entry team stayed close to the door and allowed the dog to meander down the corridor. He ignored the stairs that lay on his right; the first door was to his left, and it led to a large dining room with a bay window that overlooked the front of the house. The dog crossed the threshold of the room, sniffed around the table and chairs, and then turned back into the hallway; he walked up the hallway and past the understairs cupboard. An archway led into the lounge and the dog continued into the room, where he padded around the sofa and armchair sniffing the ground and the air as he went but finding nothing of interest. The four members of Bravo Team stepped into the hall and followed behind. At the rear of the house was the kitchen, Bravo group stopped at the entrance to the lounge and Jim stared at the screen. The dog was in the kitchen now. He walked slowly across the floor, head down sniffing hard, his senses taking in the variety of smells leading him to the sink; he ignored the tempting smells from the pantry and the bowl of water on the floor. Doug had seen the bowl of water as well and was hoping that Buzz would not be tempted to seek out the cat or dog that obviously lived there. After inspecting the back door, and a brief time at the well-used cat flap, Buzz turned around and headed back into the lounge. Jim and his team pressed their backs against the wall of the hallway and allowed the dog to pass them. The dog was a veteran, he knew that he needed to inspect the rooms upstairs. He glanced at the team as he passed and began to ascend the stairs, taking them slowly, one at a time. Halfway up he stopped, cocked his head to the right and lifted his ears. Doug turned to Jim, who was on his shoulder, and tightened his hold on the lead.

"He's on to something," then turned back to the dog and waved him on.

Jim gave his men a nod and pressed the mike with his thumb and whispered, "Stand by. Looks like the dog thinks we have something upstairs, nothing on the screen yet but he's reacting to something."

The team edged along the hallway and made their way to the foot of the stairs, the dog began to move again but stopped when he reached the ultimate step. The stairs went straight to the landing with no dog leg, so Jim and his team's view was unobstructed apart from Doug and Buzz who was about five metres out on the lead. The dog had not made a sound, and the team was impressed. The dog's senses were on red alert, and working overtime bought a familiar smell into his nostrils. He sniffed the air and caught the scent as it drifted towards him. He swivelled his head and looked back at the men who stood at the foot of the stairs; their presence was all the encouragement he needed. He stepped onto the landing and followed the unmistakable scent of a dead body. There were three bedrooms on the floor, each with a door that was ajar. The dog sniffed at the first two doors but ignored the rooms. At the door of the third one his tail jumped to attention, and he stepped gingerly into the room. The camera on his head was at the perfect angle to pick up the body that was slumped on the floor, the pool of congealed blood on the floor by the head was confirmation to the men downstairs that there was no threat present. They moved up the stairs in single file, passed the bedrooms that were unoccupied with caution, peering inside as they moved on to where the dog was, now prone looking back towards Doug. They headed methodically towards the last room, watching their footfall, keeping the silent approach towards the open door of the third bedroom. Doug pulled the lead, and Buzz came out of the room.

Passing Jim, Doug said, "Over to you old chap, I'll be on the stairs if needed."

He could see through the gap of the open door; he raised his left hand into the air, to halt the progress, and formed a clenched fist, opened the hand, and indicated to the room. Each to a man understood that the threat was in that room, and what was to happen next. He depressed the send switch on his radio, "Stand by." As he did, he felt the reassuring squeeze on his shoulder. "Go." He moved one metre into the room then stepped to his right another metre, his MP5 stuck in his shoulder following his gaze, his heart almost leaping out of the body armour, ignoring the prone shape, scanning the room for any other threats. John did the same to the left looking behind the door. As soon as John had entered, Andy scanned the doorway with his eyes and MP5 set on the lifeless figure on the floor. He felt the reassuring pressure of Paul, backed into him facing away covering the corridor, and unsearched rooms, and maintaining eye contact with Doug and Buzz, the latter chewing on an old tennis ball.

The team were set and planted and shortly afterwards the radio clicked into life.

It was Jim: "Room clear and secure."

Jim thumbed his mike again. "We have a body, entry wound in the right eye with an exit wound at the back of the skull. Looks like he has been here a while, there is no sign of life. We have a weapon on the floor, he has pushed the barrel against his eye and pulled the trigger and the bullet has done the trick. We are vacating the premises now and the boys outside can come and do their stuff. CID, it's all yours now. Alpha and Bravo meet at white one and prepare to stand down." He motioned to the door, and they headed back downstairs, the dog trotted behind them and licked his lips in anticipation of his reward.

Outside the teams breathed a sigh of relief and began to stand down, they made their way to the front of the house and found their friends.

Simon could not help himself. "Eye-Eye, what have you lot been up to then?" he asked. Gallows humour helped to relieve the stress and a few of them smiled at his feeble joke.

Phil and Reuben led the way back to the gazebo and Phil motioned towards the command centre.

"I have a few things to clear up, get the boys warm and fed and I will be back in ten for a debrief."

Reuben gave him a mock salute and led the men inside. One by one they collapsed onto the floor near their kit bags and began removing their gear.

CHAPTER FIVE

Outside the CID officers had begun to brief and organise the scene of crime officers. As the Firearms group stripped off and looked for drinks and food, the new influx of specialist officers prepared for their work. The scene would be catalogued and recorded; every inch of the house would be inspected and photographed. This would be treated as suspicious until it was decided that the poor youth had intended to take his own life, if indeed that was the case. The men inside the gazebo were relieved that their work here was done; they grabbed their tea and biscuits and devoured them. Jammy Dodgers began to fly across the room as Plymouth challenged Exeter to a biscuit battle. The biscuits flew across the room and bounced off their body armour. Some shook their heads at the childishness until they found an unopened pack then they ripped open the biscuits from the pack and joined the battle. The first shot caught Jim in the eye and the teams roared with laughter.

The teams wound down and began to look forward to a relaxing afternoon and a little down time. They were comfortable in each other's company and had forged a strong bond as they trained together. Each member had his reasons for joining these elite teams.

Jim had been a young officer in the Royal Marines who now lived in Cornwall. Cornwall and Jim were inseparable; he lived to surf. No wave was too big for him and the bigger the swell the faster his heart pumped. He would often post photos on social media whenever he had, and his son had 'hit some waves'.

The teams, almost to a man, had interests which were predominantly adrenalin based: motorbikes, fast cars, mountain biking, surfing, extensions to the roles that they undertook every day.

Simon, one of the quieter members of the group, had already stowed his kit away and took on the role of mother.

"You messy twats, look at the mess you have made!" Discarded Jammy Dodgers covered the floor of the gazebo. He turned and looked at the other team's driver, Simon T, and asked if he could borrow their van's broom, dustpan, and brush.

Simon T leant into the side of the Sprinter, pushed his hand through the open sliding door, and grabbed the broom, dustpan, and large black bin liner.

"I will help, as I don't trust you, knob."

The two Simons laughed in unison; they took the broom and began the clean-up operation.

Phil put his bags away and sat in the back of the Sprinter. He fired up the laptop and waited for it to load up, the ring tone of his job phone broke the silence, and everyone stopped what they were doing and looked towards him. Jason and Jo stood up and leant inside the van; if the job phone rang it nearly always meant something had kicked off and there was a job to be done. They were all shattered and ready to go home but they were already beginning to doubt that they were heading back to base.

As Phil spoke his facial expression changed and his body stiffened, he was nodding vigorously and scribbling in his A4 briefing book. He looked up and gestured towards the other team's leader, to join him. Jim slipped in beside him and glanced at the book. Phil lowered the phone and turned to Rick.

"Guys, I'm getting an update on a job down in Cornwall. I

know you are over time limits for carrying and have been on the go for some time but if any of you guys up for staying on it looks like it's going to be a good one."

The question did not need asking. Each team member was running on adrenalin, and there was not one who would take the chance of missing the one job that their training had prepared them for.

One by one they rattled off their replies, sixteen men all tired and ready for some rest and recuperation and not one of them wanted to go home. The pride in Phil's chest was struggling to burst out, and he could feel his heartbeat racing. His announcement had given every member a second wind; any sign of weariness had gone, and once again they were firing on all cylinders.

The two team leaders returned to the phone call and confirmed with nods and grunts that they had two full teams who were ready and willing to answer the call. Everyone was once again in automatic mode. They were kitting up in silence, knowing exactly what to do, and who had to do what.

CHAPTER SIX

Tilly Light and her twenty-six-year-old daughter Sally had lived in Wadebridge in Cornwall for about eight years, since the sudden death of husband and father, Luke in a motorcycle accident.

With a tight-knit population of just over 6000 everyone knew everyone or knew someone who did. The town was built beside the River Camel; it was popular with tourists, but not many people moved down to live there. The population had remained steady for nearly fifty years. It seemed a better place to be, far from the hustle and bustle of London, and the sad memories it held.

Tilly and Luke met many years ago whilst young pupils at a busy London Secondary School and had enjoyed each other's company, but they were young and shy and neither had the courage to ask the other one out on a date. They had left school and gone their separate ways. Luke completed his national service with the Guards and Tilly had joined a local solicitor as a typist. They met again at a local dance in Barns Green Village Hall nearly six years after leaving school. From that day forward they were inseparable.

Luke was an amiable and well-built young man, whose passion was a small bespoke furniture business, in Horsham, West Sussex which he had started upon finishing his military service.

Upon his sudden death, the business came to a grinding halt, and Tilly and her daughter, finding the death difficult to come to terms with, withdrew into their own company.

Sally had been bought up in a world of cabinet making, and meticulous attention to detail, and her father had been able to command big money for the products they produced. The reputation of the family's level of expertise travelled around the world, and their client base reflected that. The order books were full to at least three years ahead. The upshot of this was a very comfortable way of life, resulting in a succession of nice houses, holidays when they could and motorcars.

After about two years following the death of Luke, Tilly had spoken at length to Sally, about reigniting the business, more as a cottage industry, elsewhere.

Having both agreed, it was decided to buy a small unit with a house, drive and outbuildings on the side of the A39, near Wadebridge in Cornwall. Value for money, easy access and space to work were major factors. This combined with the vacation feel of the area that Luke loved so much, and where all their memories were embedded, helped in the decision-making.

Once they were set up, and had settled in, the business began to thrive; orders were reordered and they continued to put everything into a business they loved, and which held fond memories. The pain of the loss of Luke was still there but lessened as time flew by. They had taken advantage of the passing traffic which seemed to double every year, and both sensed an opportunity to earn a comfortable living again, and even took on a small, talented workforce. The business quickly gained a reputation, locally, as a typical go-to place for anything retro or avant-garde, and it flourished. Before long they added a shop and a small café and sold locally made household knick-knacks, and fancy decor.

Tilly and Sally immersed themselves in the business. They were happy in their own company and did not seem interested in partners or relationships.

They kept a tidy house and workplace. Tilly fussed over the customers and was the point of reference if you had a problem; furthermore, she was discreet and completely trustworthy. Sally was more pragmatic and industrious. She preferred to get her hands dirty and thrived on solving problems that left others scratching their heads. As difficult and awkward a problem or repair might be, Sally viewed it as a challenge and the lights in the workshop would often burn through the night. Their mother-daughter relationship worked well despite their age difference; they loved each other dearly and neither could bear the thought of losing the other.

CHAPTER SEVEN

Their November 5th began like every other day as they went about their daily chores as they had done a thousand times. Tilly and Sally were busy opening the workshop. Tilly set about sorting out the day's tasks; she checked the shop's display shelves and jotted down any shortages as she went. Sally headed out to the workshop; there were no items in for repair, so she began a massive clean-up operation, oiling and polishing every tool and then placing it neatly on the display rack that ran for the full length of the rear wall. It was quiet all morning; customers came and went, and a few stopped for a short chat, but the majority were keen just to browse and be on their way. Tilly popped back into the house and dealt with some housework. Midday came and went without the usual rush—it was going to be a long afternoon and Sally would soon be getting hungry. She opened a fresh pack of bacon and nipped into the larder for six free range eggs. As the bacon began to sizzle under the grill, she stuck her head out of the door and gave her daughter a shout.

"Darling, come inside, it's time for lunch!" Sally did not need to be told that the bacon was almost on the plate as the smell wafted out of the kitchen and across to the workshop, she was already washing her hands when she called.

As they sat at the table and tucked into their food, the Police Firearms team, seventy miles away were all tucked up in their beds ready for the busy night ahead.

The shop and café had a large entrance straight off the A39. It was clearly signposted from approaches in both directions: 'London Lights Furniture', with the telephone number at the bottom. Sally had thought of the catchy name when they had settled in.

To anyone who ever visited the property, it was obvious that the main products could command a high retail price, although the price labels were never affixed. The one obvious legacy of Luke's influence was their passion for nice cars. In front of the workshop were their cars. Tilly had a gleaming black Mercedes four wheel drive, with trailer affixed—a practical yet expensive luxury which was only a year old. Beside it was an equally new range Rover Sport with a personal plate of SL999.

Gary had been their driver for many years, ever since they had made the move down from London, all those years ago and they all got on well. They had followed the ups and downs of his life and had held his hand with tears in their eyes when he broke the news of Marjory, his wife's, sudden death, of an aggressive cancer, some years ago. As soon as he arrived every morning, they would discuss the previous evening's Radio 4 programmes and sit and drink tea. Tilly would load the oven up with bacon and sausages and they would spend a few hours chatting. If Tilly or Sally had any heavy lifting to do, Gary was always happy to help for an hour or two before leaving to deliver or pick up. Weather and traffic allowing, he usually arrived at work between 06.30 and 07.00.

As circumstances were to unfold that evening there would be no cooked breakfast awaiting him the next morning, the 6th of November.

CHAPTER EIGHT

Gary James had driven for the Lights for years; in fact within a couple of weeks of them arriving in Wadebridge. As age had crept up on him, he made the transition from hauling heavy goods vehicles up and down the M1 corridor and settled into the more relaxed furniture delivery business. The hours were more sociable and the nights of eating and sleeping in the back of a dirty DAF were just a distant memory.

He took pride in his job; he thought of each customer as a friend and had never let any of them down on a delivery. Whatever the weather conditions and regardless of traffic hold-ups or road closures Tilly and Sally knew that their customers knew that their orders would be delivered on the day that it had been promised. When things did not go well, he only needed to roll down his window to enjoy the stunning coastline and countryside that came with the job.

Having left the world of long-distance driving, he sat down with his wife Marjory and told her that he loved driving, and he loved this part of the world; the best paid job that gave him the freedom he yearned for was the driving. She had spent many nights worrying about him and was delighted that he wanted to live, work and drive in Devon and Cornwall. The couple agreed that the last of their money should be spent on the training courses that Gary would need to complete. For nine long years they had lived happily in sleepy Wadebridge with Gary leaving for work at five and rarely returning home later than five in the afternoon, In the evening they would wander down to their local for a steak and a pint or sit on the veranda of their bungalow and watch the world go by.

In March 1998, Gary had returned home with a smile on his face and a huge bunch of Cornish daffodils in his hand. The house was quiet. There was a low-pitched whine coming from the kitchen, and he knew that something was wrong. His heart sank, and his stomach churned as he stepped under the archway into the kitchen. His Labrador Ralph sat bolt upright in the middle of the floor; next to him was the body of Marjory. A cup full of tea had fallen to the floor and smashed on the tiles. There was no crime, his wife had simply died because of a massive aneurism, dead before she hit the floor the doctors had told him—he thanked God for small mercies. Despite the heartbreak, he kept driving. For a year or so, Ralph travelled with him and kept him company as he drove up and down the roads and motorways, but those days had long since passed as Ralph's health declined with old age. The dog, the Lights, and his customers with the beauty of the southwest were the only things that kept him from taking one of his old hunting rifles and blowing his head off.

Now he slept without female company, and every night Ralph would leap onto the bed snuggle down under the duvet. Last night Ralph had buried his head deeper searching for sanctuary as the fireworks rose above the bungalow.

As usual he was awake long before the alarm sounded. He welcomed it with grunt, while Ralph twisted and growled under the covers as his deep sleep was disturbed.

As he dressed and cleaned his teeth Phil and the rest of the police teams were over an hour away, oblivious to Wadebridge and the impending events, wiping the Plymouth frost from their sleeves. They did not know each other but would meet for the first time before the sun went down and Gary's life would change forever.

Ralph poked his head out of the covers and rested his neck on the pillow imploring his owner to allow him an extra few minutes of warmth and security. Gary shook his head and grinned; he threw the covers to one side, got out of bed and patted Ralph on the head.

"Sorry old boy, we have to earn a living," he joked.

Their routine was always the same. Ralph eventually dragged himself out of the warm bed and plodded downstairs to be greeted by a warm kitchen and welcome bowl of icy water. The Aga ran continuously ensuring the old bungalow was a comfortable, homely place for them. Gary showered and shaved then followed his best friend down into the kitchen and popped the kettle onto the hot plate. While it boiled, he patted his face and hair with an old tea towel.

"How was your night?" Gary asked. Ralph ignored the question and pawed at the pantry door, awaiting the arrival his breakfast.

Gary opened a tin of Pedigree's finest dog food and spooned it into Ralph's bowl; he added half a cup full of left-over gravy to encourage Ralph to eat. Ralph caught the scent of the Bisto and devoured the lot. Gary was not and never had been a breakfast man. Mainly because he knew that in a few hours, his Tilly would be frying up some bacon and eggs and stuffing it inside a few slices of fresh Cornish bread. Thinking about it made him hungry, and his stomach rumbled in anticipation.

He squatted down, and softly grabbed Ralph by his collar. They were mates—good mates, and they looked at each other, as they did every morning.

Gary spoke. "Well friend, I'm off. Be good, chill out and I'll see you later… I might even get some goodies for us both tonight if you behave yourself. No eating the sofa while I am away, please and if the postal worker comes, please don't attack the front door." Ralph stared back at him and prepared to run back to the bedroom and dive under the covers.

He closed the door and left, walking up the side alley to where his push bike leant against the doors of his shed. It was sheltered from the early morning frost, but the steel handlebars were still icy cold. As he crunched along the shale walkway, he made a mental note to put it right in the summer, the noise it made every morning and the way it attracted every cat in the neighbourhood drove him mad. The heady aroma of cat piss was everywhere especially on cold mornings.

He tucked his jeans into his socks and strapped on the ridiculous helmet that Marjory had always insisted he wore. He unlocked the gate and pushed the bike onto the driveway, then he swung his leg over the crossbar and cycled out on to the main road, up to the T-junction and then turned left on the small track that ran alongside of the A39 towards Tilly and Sally's, which was gentle ten-minute cycle away. He glanced over shoulder to his left and caught a glimpse of his bungalow. A small light illuminated the front bedroom window, the unmistakeable shape of Ralph sat watching him, patient as always, not making a fuss, looking down the road, watching as his master began his cycle to work. As soon as he was out of view Ralph would be in the bed and fast asleep, he chuckled and began to pump the pedals.

His meeting with Tilly and Sally and the inevitable bacon and egg bap was only half an hour away, at a steady cycle.

He generally knew the day before where he may be driving,

but this week was quiet, and he expected to bumble around the shop and outhouses and have an easy but still enjoyable day. His stomach let out a deep growl. He smirked and licked his lips, subconsciously speeding up: today's breakfast will be a welcome start. He was also eager to discuss the previous evening's comedy series on the radio.

CHAPTER NINE

Tilly had set the two alarms as she had done thousands of times before. She always placed them out of the reach, negating the opportunity to cancel the chime, and roll over. The long days ensured that she and Sally seldom had sleepless nights and were oblivious to the odd vehicle that either drove past or used the drive as a turning circle.

Sally's eyes opened and blinked in the dark room. For a moment she was a little confused. Turning over on her left side, she sat up and strained to see the luminous dial of one of the clocks on the bureau at the bottom of the bed. She blinked and rubbed her eyes.

"Two o'clock," she murmured. She felt uneasy; she could not put her finger on it, but she felt something was not quite right. Turning over away from the clock she squeezed she called to her mum who slept next door.

"Mum, mum, wake up." She spoke in a quiet, deliberate voice. Her eyes were becoming accustomed to the light

"What's… what's wrong love?"

Their bedroom doors had been left ajar as usual.

"schuh, I think someone's outside."

Sally had not heard anything for sure, but she had an uneasy, almost sick feeling in the pit of her stomach.

Without a word, Tilly quietly sat up, shifting her feet to the floor, and into the neatly positioned slippers. She suddenly froze, noticed the silhouette of someone or something through the nets pass the window. She stood up, eyes fixed on the window, unblinking.

She spoke deliberately, and slowly. "Sally, my love probably nothing, but after I've left the room, close your door and put your slippers and dressing gown on. I won't be long."

Sally did not say anything but watched the area of her open door and watched as her mother passed in the hallway. As she closed her door and turned back towards her bed, she saw the dark shape outside, crouched and moving slowly outside the window. Her heart was racing.

"Mum!" she shouted, whilst turning her head towards the closed door where Tilly had been. She glanced at the window; the shape had gone, and her thoughts centred on her love. *Be careful Mum, be careful.*

Tilly was standing still outside of the Bedroom door. She stared down the corridor which led directly to the front door, unblinking. She could also see the doors that led off the corridor. Squinting she focused on a boot mark on the red tiled floor, straining to hear anything, something, hoping her mind was playing tricks. Her heartbeat quickened and pounded in her ears

There was someone or something in the house. She was not afraid; rather, it was the not knowing mixed with adrenalin. She feared for her beloved Sally, whom she hoped had done as she had asked.

Tilly felt an icy cold breeze against her bare ankles. *One of the doors is open* she thought. They had locked all the doors before they had gone to bed earlier in the evening. Her mouth was dry, and she hesitated. It seemed liked minutes but was only a matter of seconds. Tilly turned sharply, back towards their bedroom, to where Sally was alone. As she did, she felt a force strike her in the back, with a deafening noise. It seemed that

59

someone had turned all the lights out as her body hit the ground with such speed and force that she did not have time to put either of her arms out in front of her. Her face smashed into the ceramic floor tiles shattering her nose and breaking all her front teeth. The blackness had engulfed her before she hit the ground.

Sally had been at the foot of the bed, with the bed between her and the closed door, when the shot rang out causing her to cup her ears.

"Mum! Mum!" she shouted towards the closed door. As she did, the bedroom window behind her exploded showering her with glass. She fell forward onto the bed, bouncing off on to her back on the floor. As she lay there, she could feel the wetness under her, and the metallic taste of blood in her mouth. She propped herself up, and saw something parting the nets, which were bellowing out in the gusting wind. Her mind was racing, and as she tried to turn, she winced as a pain the likes of which she had never experienced shot up from her thigh to her shoulder. She was struggling to breathe as her mouth filled with blood. Clawing at the duvet, she pulled herself up and looked at the window. There it was, a figure, a dark-coloured figure, half in and half out, with one leg on the bedroom floor extending an arm out to the frame for support. The other arm extended out pointing at her. *What was that? A gun!*

The shot that had struck Sally jarred Tilly back into the here and now. She was winded and knew then that she had been shot. There was no feeling in her legs, and she tried to raise her head from the floor, out of the bone and mulch that had been her nose and teeth. Tilly sensed something was behind and above her and glanced towards the bedroom door.

Sally! I must get to her.

The figure in the window fell awkwardly inside on to the

floor, behind Sally. She saw the person reach for something to stop the fall, in doing so dropping what was in their hand. Her eyes darted to where the gun had fell, it was a shotgun, and her mind filled with dread.

The pain hit Tilly like a bolt of lightning, but she could not really understand what had happened, and for a split second she thought she had fainted. She brought her arms up under her chest and raised her head slightly, turning to the left. As she did, she felt something at the back of her head forcing it roughly down, on to the cold tiles and into the blood, and shit that were her teeth. Tilly's eyes flickered and winced at the pain, as she drifted off into the darkness again, but before she blacked out, he knew what it was that was forcing her down: it was a boot, someone's boot!

Sally had the advantage, as her eyes were accustomed to the darkness, and could see the dark figure scrambling in the broken glass to find the weapon they had dropped.

She tugged hard on the quilt towards the figure, and it fell on him, she tugged again, and the shape disappeared thrashing under the bedding. The pain she felt was intense, and she felt sick. She knew she had been shot, and that her mum was probably injured or worse outside the door. Her best chance was to get away, to get help, to help Mum. As she pulled herself up, she realised that her nightgown had been torn by the blast at the base of her back. The shot had been an instinctive random shot mostly missing Sally's back and embedding dozens of tiny pellets and associated debris, into the wall at the head of the bed. The plasterboard had imploded in a hail of plaster paint and wood, leaving a thin cloud which was settling quickly. Sally fell on to the figure under the quilt beating the struggling form with her clenched fists. She gritted her teeth, trying to find the head underneath the bedding. Holding it down with her left hand she landed blow after blow, on the skull of the person, who was trying to harm her and her mother.

Without warning Sally was struck with something from under the mass of curtains and netting. The blow caught her right eye, knocking her off the crouched figure. Stumbling to get up, she turned towards the door.

"Mum! I'm coming!" she called out, and attempted to run, slamming into the bedside cabinet, and falling to the floor.

As she rose, a hand grabbed her hair from behind, pulling it sharply backwards. Flinging both arms up she grabbed the arm and felt the strong vicelike grip from a hand which was gloved. Pulling her head forward and to the left, she caught a glimpse of a leg in jeans.

Tilly's head spun, and she felt weak. The pressure from the boot on her head had eased, and she opened her eyes. She was finding it difficult to breathe and struggled to spit out the crap that was in her mouth. She raised her head slightly. The figure was squatting on her, and it was heavy. Her ears were ringing but she could hear shouting, it was male's voices. She tried to call out. "Sally, Sally run!" but the figure pushed down on her head and a head came close to hers.
"Shut up you stupid bitch, or we will finish the both of you off; where's the fucking safe?"

Sally heard her mum, and made for the door, where she rose and turned. In front of her between the window and the door, was a huge male figure, all in dark clothing. He had pulled off all the fabric and netting from the windows, and she could clearly see the glaring eyes, which drilled into her from the black ski mask.

His arms were extended to his front. He was holding a

shotgun and it was levelled at her chest.

Sally's head was throbbing, and she could hardly catch her breath; her mind was confused and for a second, she was frozen to the spot. Her head darted to the left and the closed door. It was the only thing that stood between her and her mum.

"Don't even think about it," said the man, and she turned to him. Sally was frightened, really frightened, and for a second did not know what to do. She needed to get to her mother. The stalemate seemed like an eternity but was in fact seconds. It was like Sally's body moved before she knew what she was doing. She flung herself towards the figure and let out a high-pitched scream, her arms flailing to get the gun.

The flash and sound of the twin barrels caught Sally by surprise, as she felt herself being hit in her chest with a force that lifted her and smashed her into the closed door.

As she slid to the floor, her life ebbed away with the blood into the carpet.

Tilly opened her eyes, and a tear rolled down her cheek. The figure above her shouted something, and there was a reply from the bedroom area. Tilly felt nothing and her mind pictured Luke and young Sally hand in hand smiling to her, beckoning to her.

A smile worked its way through the blood and torn skin, as she breathed her last, and felt herself slipping away.

The boot on Tilly lifted off, and the figure stooped down. A gloved hand turned her head to one side. Her eyes remained open, but the life was gone. He stood up and turned towards the corridor that led to the bedroom.

He called out, "Michael, get your arse in here."

The door to Sally's bedroom opened, and the tall figure walked towards where Tilly lay. The two men faced each other, with the guns at their side. Tilly's murderer looked down at her body then up at the other figure. He raised his left arm up, and grabbing the mask took it off, placing it in his overalls breast pocket. The other male did the same. Thomas Burns was sweating and licked his lips; his mouth was dry. Michael, his twin brother, looked down at the body on the floor, and opened the shotgun he was carrying, removing both spent cartridges, and placing them in his pocket. He tutted, and then giggled, looking at his twin Thomas.

"Fuck bruv, we've done both of em."

Michael nodded. "Are you sure she's finished?"

Michael beckoned to Thomas for him to follow. As they entered the bedroom, Sally was splayed out on the floor, her body broken by the blast. Thomas stared at the young girl, and then gestured to Michael.

"Check the pictures in here and the lounge and look behind them, there must be some sort of safe somewhere. Find the keys for the motors as well."

Michael went to the furthest wall and turned to Thomas. "Give the others a shout, they can come and get the cars, and wait for us in the lane."

Thomas took out a mobile and tapped in a number, it rang and was answered almost at once.

"Yep, it's me. Come into the lane."

CHAPTER TEN

Gary was enjoying the ride into work. He had not met any other vehicle, which was not unusual. There was a slight damp in the air which tickled his throat as he inhaled. He glanced down at his watch, and noted it was getting lighter. Gary glanced up and saw the gates up to the right and slightly ahead. He stopped and planted both feet on the ground. Something puzzled him, he thought, and then it struck him: there are no lights on!

His stomach rumbled again; maybe they had slept in, or a fuse has gone.

Getting off the bike he walked over to the main entrance. As he did, he noticed that neither car was there. In all the years he had been working there, there was always one of the ladies to be found, normally indicated initially by whose car was outside. Approaching the front of the house, he noticed it was quiet, quiet. Settling his bike against the antique water pump, he stood and looked around. He noted the deep tread marks from where the two cars normally parked leading down the drive. He had an uneasy feeling but did not know why. Before he walked up to the door, he took out his mobile and tapped in Tilly's number and rang it, but it went straight to answer phone. Cancelling it, he immediately rang Sally's. He lowered the mobile as he strained to hear a ringtone coming from within. As he cancelled the call, the ring also stopped.

Everything inside of him was telling him not to be stupid, but the fear that something was wrong was growing, and making him nervous. Looking to his left he saw the rake, which was used to tidy the drive. Reaching over he picked it up. *Just in case,* he thought.

Walking up to the front hallway, he glanced to the right, and saw the window to Sally's bedroom, apparently open, with a net curtain draped outside. Pausing he raced through the what-ifs, and it did not make sense. *Where are the cars? Why aren't the lights on? Why is no one here? Why... please let everything be okay.*

Suddenly he caught a smell. He paused, inhaling through his nose, then he raised his head slightly. The smell was faint but was there nonetheless it was there. Momentarily he could not think what it was. He sniffed again and closed his eyes and then it dawned on him. The last time he had smelt that it was on a local charity event, at a clay pigeon shoot. It was the smell you get when you fire a gun!

Gary's heart raced, as he knew that neither of the women owned any guns of any description. They disliked weapons of any sort. He instinctively crouched, although it was almost fully daylight, and holding the rake across his body, edged towards the open window.

As he peered in, his view was obscured by the net curtain. Extending the handle of the rake, he hooked the curtain and drew it to the side of the window. Through the window his eyes followed the end of the bed, and up towards the open door. Initially he could not make out the heap against the bottom half of the door, and he edged closer. Squinting he drew back with a sudden gasp, dropping the rake. Through the light he had made out the seated figure of Sally, her head hung down to one side, with her back against the door. The door behind was shattered and sprayed with what appeared to be blood. Gary backed away and lost his footing, crumbling to the floor, instinctively scrabbling to get up, to get away, far from here. As he tried to rise, he gagged, but nothing but bile filled his mouth. As he ran down the drive, his left hand fumbled under his waterproof jacket for the little-used mobile. His thoughts were scrambled, and he did not know what to do, or where to run to. He fell again, and the phone spun out of his hand on to the drive. Grabbing it he rolled to his left behind the Devon Bank that hid him from view and bordered the A39. His hands trembled, and he was sick. The image of

Sally was constantly there, and he closed his eyes. He had the phone to his ear, as he heard the female's voice asking him what service he needed. He hesitated, again the female asked what service he wanted.

Gary replied hesitantly at first.

"Police… Police quick, please, quick!" and he started to sob.

CHAPTER ELEVEN

Years of training and practising, drills and rehearsals had embedded the skills into the minds of the Firearms teams. Phil's team based in Exeter, and Simon's team in Plymouth, thought as one. Each team duplicated the other in roles and responsibilities.

The distinctive ring tone of the Exeter team's phone echoed out and each head raised, straining to listen to the conversation. Phil listened intently to the call nodding his head.

"Lads heads-up please. Plymouth boys stand fast, my team, three plus me in the four-by-four, the remainder in the van." Phil leaned towards Simon. "Clear up here mate and stand by to stand by." Simon nodded. Striding over to the car, and van, he could hear the team checking, and double-checking. In the car was Jason, Rick and Tim, who was the driver. Reuben was to drive the van, with Brian riding shotgun. The boys had ensured that the flasks in the van had been filled with fresh boiling water. The Plymouth lads had kindly passed over a large assortment box of broken biscuits.

Tim gunned the car and looked in the rear-view mirror. Silhouetted were the large figures of Rick and Jason in the back, bulked out by the two stones of body armour and kit. The limousine-tinted windows denied him the ability to give the thumbs up to the boys in the van and recognise any response. Looking to his right he moved the wing mirror, so that he had a clear view of Reuben, in the driving seat of the van. Reuben could see him, and he raised his right thumb, as did Tim. Closing the window, and adjusting the mirror, they moved off in convoy, out of the car spaces, and headed to the T-junction.

Phil had punched in the postcode to the farm shop in Wadebridge, the powers that be in the Control in Exeter, were busy looking at computer maps of the area and trying to find the best and safest place to use as a meeting point, or rendezvous point.

Phil had consulted with Simon, from the Plymouth team, and Reuben, about a position to stop upon arrival. Phil would play it by ear, and upon arrival, would relay the info to everyone.

Tim hammered the Range Rover, rapidly leaving the Sprinter van behind. Communications between all the vehicles was constant. At the speeds, they were reaching leaving Plymouth, the cars would relay possible or potential hazards, negating any chance at all an accident. This time of the morning, combined with the sirens and lights meant a rapid route taking them on to the A38, and towards Cornwall.

Tim was making substantial progress, as was Reuben in the Sprinter, but they had long lost eye contact. Reuben estimated they were about ten minutes behind.

Phil was speaking to the Control Room inspector. A divisional superintendent had been nominated, with the responsibility of co-ordinating the operation, and he was based in Padstowe, only five miles along the river, from the shop. The superintendent was called Nick Jones, and Phil had known him since he was a young sergeant. He had been a firearms officer, when he was a constable, and sergeant, but had to leave with the commitments of an accelerated promotion. He was one of those officers who were destined to elevate to the dizzy heights that Phil could only dream of, and in fact was not interested in. Despite this Nick had not forgotten his roots and the people he had worked alongside. In this environment, it made for a very necessary, and solid relationship, and understanding, having been there, and literally got the T-shirt.

The vehicles were eating the miles up, and the drop-off point was close. Each member had quietened now, weapons in hand, staring into space, embroiled in their thoughts, running over positions, responsibilities, and what-ifs.

The Range Rover slowed, and Tim turned the lights off, the early morning mist had dispersed, and as he leant forward and squinted, he looked right at the Devon bank that edged the road.

Phil put his phone down.

"Guys we're here. Tim pull across the road on our offside and stop."

Traffic had been stopped on the opposite approach by traffic officers, and as they pulled across the road, he could see the entrance about seventy-five metres ahead and to the left. As he scanned across the drive, he also could see the top half of the shop, and outbuildings.

Phil's radio crackled into life.

"Pulling up behind now, boss."

It was Simon and rest of the team in the van. Looking in the nearside mirror, Phil saw the van edge up to the rear, and the sliding side door slowly open.

One by one Phil and his team exited the car, crouched, and silent. He went around the front of the car, and beyond for about fifteen metres, to enable a two-team form up, an exercise they had practised hundreds of times. As each of the drivers exited last, they placed their keys on the rear offside tyre, under the wheel arches a very necessary action in case any member required to get access, for any reason.

Scanning ahead Phil had assumed his role as number one of

team one, the entry team.

The height of the Devon bank hid them from any view, but he could clearly see the entrance ahead of him.

Cradling his Heckler and Koch, He felt Tim close in behind, followed by a squeeze on top of his left shoulder. Without a word or the need to look behind, he knew that both teams were in position, and keyed his send button.

"From Phil, radio check over."

In quick deliberate, and quietened the voices replied, "Tim okay, Rick okay, Jason okay."

"Alpha Team roger; Bravo Team radio check."

"Simon okay, Mick okay, Reuben okay, Brian okay."

Phil acknowledged the replies.

"Simon, Bravo Team go forward and cover the front drive." Keeping his weapon to his shoulder, he scanned the area to the front and right, keeping both eyes open. There was no need to activate the powerful torch, which hung under the stock of his now extended carbine. The effective red dot sight, darting from one place to another as he scanned was more than enough. Bravo Team passed to his left. Four members crouched, moving silently as on. Simon at the front with his weapon up, Mick, his number two, was looking to the right. Behind him with his stubby shortened Remington shotgun, was the entry man Reuben, with tail-end Charlie, Brian, scanning to his left.

Phil nodded, pleased with the way in which Simon controlled the team, and at that point thought that he could not want for a better back up team.

As Simon's team went to ground either side of the drive, he raised a thumb, and an OK sign.

"From Phil, Alpha move." In unison they started to move forward, keeping their eyes and thoughts focused. As Phil and his team reached the entrance, they passed Mick and Brian on the edge of the drive. Alpha Team passed, and Phil stopped, dropping to one knee. Looking across the drive, he spoke on the radio: "Simon, all clear, remain here. Team Alpha go, go."

The team turned into the drive continuing at a crouch, methodically, deliberately.

Phil felt his breathing quicken, and his goggles started to steam up; raising his hand, he pulled them away from his face slightly. The freezing air immediately cleared them.

Simon watched as Alpha Team moved up the drive. As good as they were, he cringed at the sound of the crunching underfoot, as the team walked on the shingle. He tutted, as he wondered why anyone would ever want this stuff surrounding their house.

Phil stopped at the old water pump, beside the bike that had been propped up, the bike belonging to Gary. Looking back, Phil's nose brushed up against the MP5, which was raised by Tim, rock steady, and aiming forwards.

Returning his gaze to the house, his attention was drawn to the window on the right with the curtains swaying in the slight breeze. The window had been smashed.

Within twenty strides, Phil and Team Alpha were set up to the left of the main entrance. Leaning slightly forward, and to his left, he saw that the door appeared closed. Rick at number three was this team's entry man, should he be needed. Phil extended his left hand and grabbed the handle. His right hand held the stumpy MP5 steady, pointing forward. Pulling the handle down slowly he pushed it and the door eased open silently. Changing hands on the weapon, he raised his right hand above him, and gave the hand opening signal, which informed the team stacked behind that the door was open.

The radio crackled: "Simon from Phil, door is open, bring

Bravo Team up now."

"Roger," replied Simon.

Bravo Team moved up, until Simon was at the heels of Alpha Team's last man Jason. He leant forward and squeezed his shoulder, and he in turn squeezed the shoulder in front of him, eventually Phil felt the same signal.

This was it, he thought. *No going back now.* He rose slightly the three figures of Team Alpha, did the same. Opening the door, he immediately entered at speed, to his left. The pattern was in one metre, and step to the left one metre. As he did so, the next man Tim did the same but to the right, dynamic room dominance. As soon as Tim was in, the large figure of Rick stamped into the frame of the door, weapon scanning the front, up the hallway, towards the kitchen, each of their weapons' red dot lasers scanning the dark recesses, threat points and beyond. Backed on to Rick, but facing out into the drive was Jason, negating any threat from behind them, his right leg stretched back reassuringly touching Rick's. A complete team, covering all angles, all working silently in unison.

"Simon, Alpha Team to enter, Bravo Team stay firm," said Phil.

"Roger," came the reply.

Phil remined at the door entrance as Tim edged down the right-hand side. He got to the first room on his right and knelt. Phil also edged down with Rick behind him, moving past the room on the right whose door was closed. As the two of them reached the end, they stopped, and Phil could see clearly into the kitchen area. About three metres in front of him on the floor was what appeared to be a body; he guessed it was a mature female.

She was face down, with her head pointing towards the team, and she was wearing a dressing gown. She was lying in a large pool of blood; it was obvious there had been a struggle in the kitchen. There were pots, pans, and utensils everywhere. Drawers had been opened, with their contents on the floor.

Phil decided to bring Bravo Team in to search the first room as they entered, the one Tim was guarding. Once this had been communicated, the other team moved up, and as soon as Tim felt the familiar squeeze, he moved up and joined Phil, who indicated with his right hand to the body on the floor. Looking around, Tim nodded.

Bravo Team opened the door which led into what was Tilly's bedroom, and entered, leaving man number four in the doorway looking towards Phil.

"Clear," came the report from Simon, and his team exited and stacked in the corridor, leaving the door open.

Phil entered the kitchen passing the prone figure on the floor, to the left. Tim entered on the right. Beyond the kitchen and again on the right was another room, with the door opening into it. Tim pointed down and to his left, at Lily's lifeless body. Rick edged in and swung his weapon across his body, kneeling beside her. Reaching down he moved her hair slightly. It was matted with blood, which was sticky and dry in places. Placing two fingers on her neck he felt for a pulse, and closed his eyes, straining to feel anything. His pulse was beating hard, and made it difficult, to concentrate. Bringing his head down to hers, he could see her eyes firmly closed, and the area around her nose and face shattered. Turning her head with his left hand, he opened her left eyelid, to be met with a bloodshot lifeless eye which was staring ahead. This is all he needed to know. Phil was behind and to the left of Tim and could see what he had done. Speaking via a throat mike, he called up, "Simon from Phil. One times deceased female, in kitchen. Send update to control."

Simon confirmed the message and fingered the second radio he was carrying, relaying the message.

Simon's team then backed on to Alpha Team, allowing the first team to approach the second door, Tim was closest, so automatically became the first person to position himself at the open door. Phil and the other members were stacked behind him, each awaiting the familiar squeeze; as he felt it, Tim entered to the right, followed closely by Phil on the left. The scene that greeted both officers was sickening.

Tim had trod on Sally's left leg, whose body was where she had fallen hours before, in a seating position, with her back against the bedroom wall.

A quick scan by both officers, confirmed that there were no other people in the room.

Rick bent down and raised the head of the young girl. As he did her light brown hair lifted off her chest, revealing a gaping wound, which had opened her chest like a mini explosion. He was leaning against the frame of the door but pulled away sharply as he realised his elbow was resting in the spray pattern of blood and matter, which was Sally's chest on the surround and wall. Her head slumped down again and, standing up, Rick exited and knelt in the corridor.

For both teams, the search of the rest of the property, and adjoining shop, took a long time, and required another team to join them to complete the task. Ambulances and considerable resources had been mobilised as the teams searched and found the lifeless bodies. High-ranking officers had received early morning phone calls, requiring them to get into work as soon as possible. Before the teams had completed the search, an Operational name had already been allocated to the investigators. Operation Oak.

Once the search had been completed, both teams exited as they had entered, to meet the ambulance crews, and senior police officers who had arrived. It was important that initially each person, upon entering, used the same route as the two teams, to ensure that any disturbance is kept to a minimum, until the scene of crime officers had done their bit.

The paramedics and a doctor, called James Mortimer entered with Reuben and Mick leading. Doctor Mortimer lived in Wadebridge, and as well as being a general practitioner, was also on the rota, as an on-call police doctor. Although it was generally accepted that the two bodies were that of Tilly and her daughter Sally, a news blackout had been put in place until the identities could be positively proved. Local radio, and BBC stations, were already alerting the public, to a major police incident, which would be affecting traffic in the area for some time. Jim Mortimer was taken to Tilly, and he immediately confirmed it was her. Despite his medical duties kicking in, he found his brain asking a myriad of questions, for which he could not find the answers. He confirmed that she was dead, and he guessed that it had happened only a matter of hours before, certainly in the morning as opposed to the evening before but kept the thought to himself. Why? What had she done? He knew that her injuries would have been unbelievably painful, and found himself resting his hand on her back, gently, momentarily, and then he stood up.

He turned to the paramedics.

"Nothing to do here, let's go to the next one."

Reuben had gone ahead, and Mick pointed towards the bedroom. Jim walked on with the ambulance guys in tow. Peering in before he had bent down, he realised no one could have survived the injuries, and that he could see as his eyes took in the mess on the wall, behind the slumped figure whom he knew to be Sally, attractive, laughing, hardworking Sally, for God's sake!

Having examined her, he exited the room with the ambulance staff, telling them there nothing for them to do, to pass their details to the police outside, and leave then he thanked them, As he left the house, he paused and took a deep gulp of air, held it then exhaled, turning to the two Firearms Officers stood next to him.

"Their cars are gone, you know, they are always parked there," pointing to the spaces along the building where there was nothing but deep tyre ruts. "I'll do a statement later and pop it down the Police station."

Cordon tape was already up, tied to anything that was available, guarded by a tall local bobby, with a clipboard, speaking to several senior officers.

The two teams had done their bit, and they went to the vehicles which had been brought forward to the main gate.

The side door to the Sprinter was open, and there were welcome drinks being poured out. On the request of Simon, there was a wooden tray of steaming pasties, proper Cornish Pasties, being passed around. The atmosphere amongst the two teams was sombre. Everyone had been changed, and Reuben and Mick, took a pasty each, grabbed their kit bags and went out of view to the rear to also get dressed, and put everything away. Within a few minutes, all the men were together, and Phil took the opportunity to speak to them.

"Guys I just want to say, thanks for an excellent job. We train and train for jobs such as these, and when we get a couple of hours tomorrow, well digest it, and see what we could have done better, but I am chuffed with each one of you. Apparently, the victims are known, a mother and daughter. It's a robbery, and their nice cars have gone." Phil went on to say that they were required later the next day, first thing in their capacity as search officers. He expected this to be a long job. "Tomorrow will be an early start, with statements from all at base, then down to here. Tell your other halves they will not be being seeing much of you, for the next couple of months or so."

CHAPTER TWELVE

JULY 1994

Several years before, in 1994, the summer in Devon was mostly warm with long days of warmth and sunshine. With this weather came the holidaymakers or 'Grockles' as locals called them. It was not a nasty or demeaning nickname; it was just one that was used and had stuck.

Reuben had been stationed as a uniformed officer at Seaton Police Station for over a year now, since passing out of his police probation, and his twenty miles plus journey from Chudleigh would be simpler if it were not for the seemingly endless number of cars towing caravans; it made a half an hour journey into an hour or even longer. The winding road did not make for a good overtaking road, often proven by regular accidents, resulting in serious or life-changing injuries, and occasionally fatalities.

His seven-year-old Vauxhall Astra SRI was a great car for this journey, and he loved to drive it. Travelling this road twice a day, almost every day, at all hours, and in all conditions, gave him an advantage, when trying to overtake, or travel at speed. There were times when returning from nights, in the early hours where he would have to stop, and catch the morning air, through fatigue, from having worked longer shifts.

His move to Seaton from his Probationary Station at Exeter, could not have been more upsetting. The Force had a policy then, that if you served your two-year probation at an urban station, then you would be sent to a rural station afterwards, and vice versa.

Reuben had completed a remarkably successful probation and enjoyed the hectic and varied workload that he carried, at one point twenty-six ongoing crimes, to deal with.

Initially when he made his reluctant arrival at the quaint little station on the seaside hill twelve months earlier, the future looked bleak. The other five officers were a mixed bag, all with lengthy services, and all lived locally. Dinner breaks were extended and taken at home, often, on a Sunday, for most of the afternoon.

Radios and equipment were occasionally left lying around, or not taken on patrol, and it was not unusual to find the night turn officer wrapped up in blankets in one of the unlocked cells, with an alarm clock and radio beside them. But that is the way it was, and had been for years, and he was not about to rock the boat. Reuben's plan from the start was to do his compulsory two years, apply for a place on an advanced driving course, and join the Traffic Department at Exeter. Being stationed at Seaton did not curb his thirst for nicking villains, and being on the border with Dorset laid the foundation for a host of cross-border crime and travelling criminals.

He got on well with his opposite number at Axminster, an officer he had joined up with: Neil Horn. Neil had also brought with him his lust for proactive policing, which occasionally pissed off the overweight, underworked, uninterested bobbies at both stations. Their joint arrest rates soon embarrassed the others; some were even secretively jealous, but none said anything.

Being so remote, bought home the very real dangers of working on your own. Reuben and Neil both had extensive military service, with Neil having been a dog handler in the RAF, and Reuben having served in the Royal Marines. Their combined experience and confidence made for a rock steady and humorous partnership, with a lot of ribbing, and rivalry, essential in remote and difficult locations. There was no such thing as satellite navigation then, so a large, waterproofed map book was essential, combined with an increasing local knowledge data base. If lost or stuck, the local inhabitants were always willing to help, and everyone knew everyone.

Police forces nationally were becoming increasingly concerned at the amount of knife and gun crime, although predominantly this was emanating from the large municipal Forces such as the Met, Greater Manchester, West Mids., to name a few. Devon and Cornwall have five hundred miles of coastline, which borders a mainly rural force. The main arterial route into the Force is the M5, which reduces to A and B roads heading into Cornwall. The cities within the Force area also attract the large criminal groups, which seem to find the geography easy to navigate, with an ever-expanding customer base for the proceeds of crime, and drugs. With this criminality comes the use of weapons of all sorts. The proliferation of a farming communities brings with it the increase in ownership of shotguns, and other firearms. Most are legal, and securely stowed away. The tragedy of the Hungerford Massacre on the 19th of August 1987, with a lone shooter Michael Ryan, in which seventeen people, including Ryan, died, and a further fifteen lay injured, prompted the Firearms (amended) Act 1988. This helped in reducing the number of firearms in private hands, most importantly handguns. Criminals resorted to obtaining firearms because of targeted burglaries, especially in rural areas.

A succession of governments realised this, and encouraged and condoned police forces to conduct regular amnesties for the collection of weapons such as knives and firearms.

CHAPTER THIRTEEN

Sunday the 10th of July 1994 was especially warm, and Reuben's bedside alarm sprung into life at just after midday. The new shifts of nights straight into late turn was a killer. The warm tacky evening had not helped him sleep well and felt like he had not slept at all.

Sarah, his wife, had got up with their young son, and left early to visit her mother, and sister, for lunch. This was a normal occurrence, to enable him to get some shuteye, ready for the long day ahead. He very rarely slept well, and the general feeling amongst the officers working this shift was that it would change, due to the drain on them. His routine was set in concrete. Up at twelve, shit, shower, change, and on the road for one, getting him to work in time to get changed and briefed.

Sundays at Seaton were very often a casual affair. The early turn officer would invariably have gone to his or her own house for a long Sunday dinner, before coming back to finish at five, ensuring there is always an overlap.

Parking the silver Astra in the designated bay on the steep hill beside the station, Reuben keyed in the code, and entered. Climbing the short set of stairs, he heard the radio transmitting from the desk of the early turn officer. Turning into the parade room, he was greeted by kit strewn everywhere nestling amongst dirty cups, out-of-date milk, and an absence of any early turn officer.

Sitting down at his desk, he noticed a yellow note taped to

his calendar. Unfolding it he recognised the writing of David, the local Special Constable. It said that he was to ring a Mrs Koenig with an address between Seaton and Axminster, and a telephone number, but did not say why.

Picking up the phone he rang the number, and after a long ring it was answered.

"Hello?" said the voice at the other end. Reuben explained who he was and that he had been asked to call. "Oh, thank you. My name is Yvonne Koenig."

Reuben could sense a slight accent, German?

"My husband passed away six weeks ago, and I have been going through some of his things. I have got something I think you may want to see."

Reuben hesitated. "Mrs Koenig can I ask what it is?

She replied that if he were not busy, she would rather show him, if that was okay. They agreed a time, and Reuben said that he would be there. Thanking her, he put the phone down. He then rang the control room at Exeter to ask to be booked on and asked if they had anything for him. As they did not, he said that he would be mobile on patrol if required with a few jobs to clear up.

Within half an hour, he was unlocking the marked police car, which was parked behind his own car. As he started the car, he looked down and cursed to himself as he saw that the night turn had only left half a tank of fuel. *Lazy bastards*, he thought.

Driving up to the top of the hill, he turned left, past the Parrot pub, and onto the Esplanade. It was quiet for a Sunday in July. Looking over to his right, he saw that the shingle beach had the odd family enjoying the weather and sea, and it dawned on him. It was changeover day at the holiday camp which he was passing on his left. The parking bays of the reception area packed with cars both arriving and leaving.

CHAPTER FOURTEEN

The drive to the address took about twenty-five minutes. Although he had passed the long entrance drive with large wooden gates, he had never been in it, or had cause to call there, and had often wondered who lived in such a large house. Leaving the car at the gates, he walked up to the right-hand side. Momentarily he looked at the polished nameplate *Le Maison*, written in ornate black lettering. It looked impressive and yet welcoming. The large double entrance gates had obviously been looked after, and enhanced the impressive first impressions, assisted by the expensive surveillance cameras set high up on each side. Pressing the intercom, Reuben awaited an answer, but was surprised when the gates started to open. Walking back to the car, he had a quick look up and down the road, got in and drove through the gates. The shingled drive reminded him of the period dramas his wife was so fond of on the TV, where they always had long sweeping drives, used by people in elegant cars. The drive was broad and lined with beautiful trees, which were all in flower, bulked out with plants and flowers of all descriptions. His window was open, and the overpowering smell of the fauna was hypnotic as it wafted in and around the car. It reminded him of the young and heady days, with his brothers, playing as kids at the base of Denne Hill, in Horsham, many years ago; happy memories. He guessed the drive was about two hundred metres long, before he was in front of the impressive property. It was as he imagined, a huge house, with large windows, and numerous chimneys. The entrance was braced either side by two large pillars supporting an entrance porchway.

Turning the engine off, he decided to leave his flat cap in the car and leant over to the back seat to pick up his folder. As he locked the car and hung the keys on his belt clasp, he glanced up and saw that the front door had been opened. There was a lady stood in the doorway, with her arms crossed looking at him, with a broad welcoming smile.

As he walked towards her, she extended her right hand.

"PC Matthews I presume?" and giggled.

"I am, indeed, Mrs Koenig; please call me Reuben. What a beautiful house, and grounds." He shook her hand and smiled back. She was taller than he expected, and had an air of being well educated, and versed in the good things in life.

"Please, my friends call me Yvonne. Come in."

Reuben followed her through the entrance hall, and down a corridor, whose walls were covered with paintings of scenery and animals. A large staircase rose to the next floors, and he followed her into what appeared to be a study, and small library.

Yvonne indicated to a soft chair, with cushions, and asked him to sit down. She sat opposite him, in a similar styled chair. "Thank you for coming PC, sorry, Reuben, I hope I have not wasted your time."

He waved his hand in a dismissive way.

"Of course not; I am intrigued."

As he spoke a man appeared in the doorway; it startled him, as he seemed to appear from nowhere.

"Reuben this is Mitch. He was a friend of my husband's and has helped on the estate for many years since leaving university about ten years ago."

Mitch walked over, Reuben stood up and shook his hand.

Mitch seemed to recognise him.

"I think we spoke some months ago, when you and your mate stopped me on the Axminster Road one night."

Reuben suddenly clicked.

"Of course, I remember now. Back light out."

Mitch laughed and explained it had been sorted. Reuben recalled that he had been a pleasant chap, that evening, and had passed a breath test.

"Can I get you a drink, hot or cold, and Yvonne?"

She politely refused, as did Reuben.

"Mitch would you please bring down the item, when you are ready; it's in the cupboard on the landing."

"Of course." he replied. "Be back in a moment."

Reuben opened his folder in anticipation and, crossing his legs, looked up at Yvonne.

"Reuben, I lost my husband to cancer about a year ago; Mitch has been a godsend. He stays here and runs the house for me. I would be somewhat lost without him."

Reuben had sensed on the phone that Mrs Koenig had an accent but could not really say what it was. She had obviously looked after herself and he guessed that her age was about seventy something.

"Yvonne I detect an accent. Is it German?"

She swept her fringe away.

"Austrian by birth. Born in a little village in the Alps just after the war, and not the First World War, before you ask." She laughed, as did Reuben. She coughed, and took out a handkerchief to stifle it, apologising.

"I'm afraid that I have a bit of a chest infection now, you'll have to excuse me. It's actually better when the weather is warm."

Reuben dismissed it. "There really is no need to apologise."

"Reuben, do you have any military experience?"

He explained about his thirteen years in the Royal Marines.

"Oh how brilliant, my husband was a military man, in fact, in a funny sort of a way, that's why I called you here." Reuben leant forward, intrigued.

Mitch came back into the room and was carrying what appeared to be a long rectangular wooden box, in his right hand, hung at his side.

"Ah Mitch, thank you; would you be so kind as to lay it down here?" she said, pointing to the carpeted floor between them. Looking down at the long slim box, Reuben was baffled as to what it may be.

"Mitch, can you pass over the photo album, in the bureau under the window, please?"

"The large black one?" asked Mitch, she nodded.

He walked over to the large window bay, under which was a broad bureau, about five feet wide, and waist height, the top of which was festooned with a wealth of photos, mainly black and white. Centre of this in pride of place, was a large art nouveau vase, in bright green and white, holding a huge bunch of assorted flowers. Yvonne had seen Reuben looking at them.

"From the garden."

Reuben said they were beautiful.

"Sarah, my wife, would love them, she is always saying I don't get her enough flowers, purely birthdays, and Valentine's Day."

She giggled, and crossed her legs, placing her hands neatly on her lap. Taking the album from him and placing it on her lap she looked up.

"Mitch, could I be cheeky, change my mind and have a black

tea. Reuben?"

"Oh okay then. White tea, no sugar, thank you."

Mitch said that was fine and left the room.

Yvonne leant forward. "Reuben, my husband, Rudi, was German, and there was a considerable age gap between us." She went on to explain that they had met when she was about twenty-three years old, and Rudi was forty, in a café in a tiny town called Witten's, just outside of Innsbruck, where she worked. She had a little waitressing job there, whilst completing her history degree at the university, which was a half-hour drive away.

"I need to tell you this, so perhaps you'll understand a little better."

Reuben nodded, and in any case, he had instantly liked Yvonne, who had a gentle, peaceful way about her. Looking at her as she pulled out a hanky, and stifled a cough, he could imagine that she had been an extremely attractive young woman, and a catch for any man of the time.

"I am sorry, I seemed to have caught, what do you call it, a bug?" she explained again.

Mitch entered the room and pulled a small table over to the side.

"Have you taken your meds?"

She held up a small pill box and nodded.

"Tea will be about five minutes," he said and left.

Yvonne gathered her thoughts and wiped her nose. "Where were we?"

She went on to explain that the attraction between her and Rudi was immediate, and that they would sit for hours talking about history and politics. She explained that she had soon realised that Rudi had served in the Wehrmacht during the war. Rudi told her that he had served as a member of the Elite

Gebirgsjäger Alpine Mountain Troops, as a sniper.

It was clear that Rudi had not been a member of the Nazi party, and in fact had chosen the Alpine Division because of the distance from Berlin, and the notable absence of Nazi diehards.

Although he rarely talked of his military career, he had been proud of what he had done, and had been highly decorated.

After they had married, they travelled the world extensively, settling in Devon, in the early seventies. Rudi's family had been wealthy farmers, allowing for a hefty inheritance, and later lifestyle.

She cleared her throat.

"Anyway I could go on forever. Rudi passed recently from abdominal cancer; he went very quickly and peacefully, which leads me to why you are here."

Mitch entered the room again, carrying the two cups of tea, passing the first to Yvonne. Reuben took his, thanked him and placed it on the floor beside his right foot, eager to open the box.

Mitch sat beside the bureau, watching intently. Seeing his eagerness, she smiled.

"Please pick up the box and see what you think."

Reuben rose and stooped to pick up the wooden box. As he raised it, he noted it felt slightly heavier than he expected.

Sitting down he placed the box on his lap, and studied it, there was no writing on it; it was dark wood, and made well, as in it was not flimsy. Noticing there were two clasps, he flicked them open. Reuben at once caught a familiar smell, but it nagged him. What was that? And then it hit him, gun oil!

With his heart pounding, he opened the wooden box. His mouth dropped open. Holding the lid open he looked at Mitch, and then Yvonne.

"Do you know what that is Reuben?" she asked.

Reuben's thirteen years career as a Royal Marine had finished as a weapons instructor, which in turn had fostered a love of military weapons, from all eras.

His brain leapt into action. "I know exactly what it is, wow!"

Within the box was an immaculate bolt action rifle, and mounted scope. It looked as new as if it had just been made.

"Can I take it out please?" Yvonne nodded then glanced at Mitch and back to Reuben.

"Be my guest."

Placing the box carefully on the floor, in front of him, he leant over and eased the rifle out of the support struts and sat back in the chair.

"Unless I am mistaken, this is a seven point nine two Walther G43 rifle, and I think ZF scope."

Pausing, he weighed up the rifle in his hands.

"Bloody hell, spot on," said Mitch.

The widow leant back and smiled.

"When we found it, Mitch researched it on the internet. It was Rudi's." She explained that before he had died Rudi had told them of the weapon's existence in a small room on the top floor. He had been issued it during the war, and had managed to hide it, and then later smuggle it into the UK, many years ago. As he had lain dying, he had explained why he had kept the rifle, and all he would say was that it had been a lifesaver on more than one occasion, during the war, and had never let him down.

Standing up, Reuben took the weapon over to the window. Holding it front of him he removed the short ten-round magazine, and noticed it was empty. Holding it in his left hand, he worked the bolt action, pulling it to the rear, and looking inside. Mitch was impressed.

"Like it?" Yvonne asked.

Reuben mimicked Forrest Gump: "I like it a lot."

Confirming the weapon was safe, he raised it to his shoulder, removed the safety catch, and gently squeezed the trigger. The trigger action was light, and there was an audible click. Lowering the weapon, he returned to the seat and sat down, with rifle across the lap.

"Mitch, I take it there's no licence for this?"

Yvonne coughed again, and Mitch offered a tissue; she leant forward and appeared to cough into the fabric held to her mouth. As she pulled it away, Reuben noticed there was blood around her mouth and on the tissue.

"Are you okay?" he asked, and, laying the rifle down, stood up to help her.

She waved him away. Standing up and looking at the tall officer, suddenly she looked frail, and her eyes were watering.

"I am sorry for being rude; I am going to have to lie down for a bit upstairs. If I can leave you with Mitch, he will brief you, and I can get in touch next week if that's okay."

Reuben said it was fine and hoped she felt better later. Turning she slowly left the room, keeping the tissue to her face; Mitch stood until she had left.

As she disappeared slowly out of sight up the long flight of stairs, Mitch sat in her seat opposite his guest.

Reuben sat down and listened intently as Mitch spoke.

"She is very ill, as you may have noticed Reuben, and it's only a matter of weeks." Mitch explained that she had been diagnosed with an aggressive form of throat cancer. She had declined any further treatment and was soldiering on as best she could. Today had been a good day. Reuben sat in silence; the excited feeling of the last hour had been crushed by this news. Slumping back, he glanced out of the window, and back to Mitch.

"Mitch, I am so sorry, she seems to really like you, and you appear very close."

Mitch looked down to the floor and cleared his throat.

"She is like a grandmother to me, and I love her a great deal." He stood up and walked to the window, crossing his arms he turned to the policeman. "Reuben I have a box of ammunition as well; can you take it all and get rid of it? I recall you have an amnesty or something going on, don't you?"

Reuben confirmed there was a weapons amnesty and explained how it worked.

"I'll need to do some paperwork, and then I will take it, okay?"

Mitch went to get the box of ammunition, and Reuben opened his folder to fill out the disclaimer. As he was writing, his mind was a tumble of thoughts. The cancer. How he wished he had met the couple before. The beautiful house, and welcome. Mitch and his love for his surrogate grandmother... it went on and on.

The disclaimer was only there to cover everyone's backs really, another waste of time, and it was another formality.

Mitch returned and handed him something wrapped up in a headscarf, Yvonne's he guessed.

"That's all of it now. I don't mean to be rude, but can I leave it to you? I'll pop up and see that she is comfortable; can you let yourself out please?"

Reuben stood and shook his hand.

"Please tell her I asked after her, and hope she feels better later. Thank you and I'll be in touch." Mitch strode out and disappeared out of view, as Reuben heard him climb the stairs.

Placing his folder on the armrest, he leant down and picked up the rifle. Placing the weapon on his lap, his mind raced back to 1986, and a beautiful afternoon on a range on the outskirts of Princetown, on Dartmoor. He, six other Royal Marines, and an American ranger were three weeks into a demanding nine-week sniper course. It was internationally recognised as arguably the hardest of its kind in any military service, worldwide, bar none. It attracted expert shooters from places such as the Middle East, and the United States. The attrition rate in the selection process alone was almost seventy per cent failure. Reuben had recently been promoted to Corporal and had already completed his weapon instructors course.

He had a clear recollection of a Sherpa van pulling up, driven by one of the course staff corporal Wallace, a chap Reuben knew from his Corps rugby days. He had jumped out, excited, and strode over to the group.

"I've managed to get me hands on a couple of bang sticks, for a play this afternoon."

Reuben giggled to himself at the phrase 'bang sticks', a light-hearted reference to equipment with one purpose, to kill.

Wally Wallace had managed to secure an afternoon of firing several weapons from the polices armoury, all of which had been used in earlier conflicts around the globe, in years gone by. One of these was a somewhat tatty but functional G43.

He recalled liking the G43 immensely. With the large amount of ammunition that had also been brought along, he ended up hitting static targets at six hundred metres. It had taken him eight rounds of the ferocious German ammunition to zero the sights in, which had put a huge smile on his face.

Reuben jolted and looked down at the weapon on his lap; he had drifted off. The room was quiet in the large house. He wondered how Yvonne was. Placing the weapon in the box he closed it and fastened the clasps.

He suddenly realised that neither of them had signed the disclaimer, and decided that could wait, he would ring tomorrow and arrange a visit again. In any case he was looking forward to spending some time with her and wanted to hear more of her life and travels.

Picking up the weapon case and paperwork, he left the room, and hesitated at the base of the stairs, hoping to catch someone's attention, but it was quiet, so he turned and left, trying not to make much noise as he strode across the gravel to his car.

He placed the weapon and paperwork in the boot, and pushed it shut, without slamming it. As he sat in the seat, he changed his status code to available on the radio, apologising for the length of time it had taken him. The radio operator replied that it had been noticeably quiet, and there was nothing for him.

As he pulled out of the drive, he indicated right to head back to the station via the Axminster Road but hesitated. Cancelling the indicator, he turned left, and drove in the direction of the coast. Within about five minutes, he was surrounded by woods, on a single-track road, and took the first left turning which was signposted Shire Water Treatment Works. Reuben had searched this area about six months previously, for a missing youth, and knew it well.

No one ever comes here, he thought to himself. At the end of the track, was a locked gate, which led to the disused, and derelict building complex. No one had been here for some years.

Turning the ignition off, he looked in the rear-view mirror. Happy that no one was coming he got out went to the boot and opened it. The radio had been quiet, and he just wanted to have another look at the rifle before the powers that be took it away, to be destroyed. He opened the boot lid, and held it open, looking at the wooden box. Again his thought drifted to that warm range day all those years ago.

He had chosen the battered G43 above the American Garand, a weapon favoured by Irish snipers during the Troubles in Northern Ireland, and the Lee Enfield 303, the weapon favoured by many Forces, and in use by many today. Arguably the best sniper rifle ever. The G43 was a legend in the hands of the highly trained Second World War German snipers, and Reuben wanted to make the most of a once-in-a-lifetime opportunity. He recalled it being forgiving, simplistic in its action, and incredibly accurate. A buzzard fighting with a crow above him snapped him back to reality, and again he smiled. Great days, which had ended in him and three others passing the course. The successful result had led him into a career of deployments as a sniper with the Royal Marines, all around the world.

Reaching into the boot, he opened the box and took out the pristine rifle. Instinct and muscle memory mad him check that the weapon was safe, and he drew the bolt back, and looked inside. *Still got it*, he thought.

Closing the boot, he looked around, and saw a path to is right, in the direction of the coast. Operating the remote, Reuben locked the car, and carried the rifle under his arm into the woods.

He missed his time in the Royal Marines and had had a promising and varied career ahead of him, but when the opportunity of a change, with better money came along, he joined the police. As he walked along, he found himself cradling the weapon, as he had been taught, and replicated the shadowy deliberate steps, he knew so well, to limit the noise, and possible trip wire, the 'Ghost Walk' as it is known. *Oh well big boys' toys,* he thought. *No one is looking, why not!*

At the end of the short track, it opened to a panoramic view of the sea ahead, and cliffs below, he crouched and edged forward, quietly, slowly, and deliberately. Glancing down he noticed the clean dry grass and sat down.

Looking to his right he could see His station town of Seaton, and its tram line to Axmouth and could make out the people and their dogs on the beach near the estuary, they were like busy ants.

Reuben was in the zone now, all the lessons, and disciplines flooded back to him; it was a game, a man's game, but a game nonetheless. He slowly shuffled around to his right and brought his knees up to support the rifle. Being righthanded, his left knee faced the town in the distance.

Judging distance was a skill long before the technology and mechanics of today, and he was an expert at it, a natural. There were several ways of calculating this and his mind was soaking up his surroundings, trying to find a target.

Looking at the tram station in the distance he could see the stationmaster, Guy, unmistakeable in his red waistcoat. Between Reuben and Guy, a valley, the Axe valley, and this gives the impression that things are further away than they are. Reuben imagined the length of a football pitch, and how many he could fit in between himself and Guy. He mentally paced it out, eight he thought, maybe eight and a half, which is eight hundred and fifty metres. A long shot by any standards, downhill as well.

Raising the rifle to his right eye, his left hand cradled the barrel and stock, and his left elbow rested on the inside of the knee. *No grip just a support*, he thought.

His right elbow fitted nice and tightly into his body.

Keeping both eyes open, he adjusted his position so that he pointed naturally at Guy, who had no idea what was happening above and behind him. *This was an exciting game,* thought

Reuben, and his heart was pounding. As he looked along the rifle it rose and dropped with every breath. The sight picture through the antiquated sight was amazingly clear and concise. The trees and bushes between them were still, and the flag above the lifeboat station hung lifelessly.

He placed the crosshairs of the German sight one notch above the distant figure of Guy, who was oblivious, and facing away, speaking with the gathering group of potential passengers awaiting the arrival of the tram.

Reuben inhaled and exhaled slowly, slowing his breathing down. Breathing in, he deliberately did it slowly then exhaled in the same way, three times.

Placing his finger on the trigger, he gently took up the pressure, he took one more breath in and out. As he inhaled again, he ensured the sight was on Guy, then held his breath, and gently squeezed the trigger. *Click*, as the firing pin shot forward. Reuben exhaled and looked through the sight. Guy continued to issue the tickets.

He lowered the weapon and placed it on the grass beside him. He fell back and laughed to himself. *Death from above,* he thought. *Death from above.*

CHAPTER FIFTEEN

He had been away from the station for about four hours and had got back to be greeted by several locals, sat in the front office. Most were regulars, concerned with things such as bonfire smoke, parking and dogs barking. He dealt with them and gave the normal advice, reassurances, and where necessary, made future appointments.

The thought of what he had done in the woods would not leave him, and he was churning over things repeatedly.

The day seemed to have rushed by and he found himself sat at his desk, fiddling with his pen, and staring out of the window. The rifle was still in the boot of the patrol car, but it needed to be placed on the amnesty register, and placed in the station's small armoury, to await removal and subsequent destruction, together with the box of ammunition.

There were no other officers on duty after him, due to the late- and night-turn officers being on last-minute holidays. This often happened in these rural stations, as the management had lost interest locally, due to the lax way things were run, and checked. They were normally the worst offenders, turning up when they saw fit, answerable to no one, and Reuben was early turn the following day. Another dreaded quick turnaround. *That was it*, he thought. *The gun and ammo can stay in the car until tomorrow.* Getting up from the worn and tattered chair, he leant down and turned the computer off at the mains. Taking off his radio, he placed it on the table and informed the control room, that he was now code eleven, which was the terminology showing he was now off duty. As it was acknowledged, he removed the radio battery and put it on charge, ready for his return a little over twelve hours away.

Leaving the station, he paused and looked back at the patrol car, with its hidden secret.

He was not worried if something happened and it was discovered, by a colleague, he would just blame it on forgetfulness, and take a telling off.

Gunning the Vauxhall down the A3052 towards Exeter, his mind was questioning his own thought process. The road was clear for an early evening, and he was revelling in the freedom to use the sporty engine, hurtling into the bendy curves of the country road. The sound of Barbara Streisand screamed from the Bose speakers in the door pockets, as his fingers tapped along on the steering wheel, mouthing the words in sync with Ms Streisand. Sarah, his wife, hated his choice of music, which harked back to his days in the Royal Marines, the late seventies, and early eighties, when music was music, with proper ballads, and meaningful lyrics. But this was his car, and today had been a good day.

He arrived home and parked outside the house, listening to the last piece of the last track, as the engine ticked over, allowing the turbo to cool down. He was looking forward to a warm welcome, hot tea and bath, and bed.

CHAPTER SIXTEEN

Reuben's alarm woke him at five, and he turned it off, and sitting up, he patted Sarah's thigh. They had gone to bed quite late, despite his intentions of having and early night. The addiction to the series *The Sopranos* was to blame, and Reuben felt it this morning. Once he had showered, he felt better, and was looking forward to the impending days off, after the next to early shifts. These earlies tended to pass quickly.

Arriving at the station car park approximately ninety minutes after waking up, he picked up his lunchbox, which Sarah had prepared the night before, and entered the nick through the side gate.

It felt like he had not been home, and everything was in its place, as he entered the kitchen and prepared the second coffee of the day and switched the kettle on.

Stirring the hot cup at the sink, he looked through the window over Seaton harbour, and the sea beyond. It was like a mill pond, and the weather forecast was clear with sunshine. Sitting at the desk, Reuben sipped from the cup, and placed on the windowsill beside him. Looking at the phone he noticed that a red light indicated there was a voice mail waiting. Having turned the power on he pressed the answer phone button, and turned the volume up.

"Message for Reuben," the message started. Reuben recognised the voice at once, it was Mitch.

"Reuben, it's Mitch; we met yesterday. I am sorry to say

Yvonne died this morning at three o'clock, I had heard her fall out of bed, or stumble, and had gone to her room to find her collapsed. There was a lot of blood; I think it was an embolism or something like that caused by the cancer, or that's what the ambulance guys, and doctor said." Mitch had finished the message by passing a telephone number, and a request that Reuben ring it when he got in.

Ringing the number straight away, it was quickly answered by Mitch, who apologised for leaving the message. He was upset, and just wanted to know, what to do, as he was on his own.

"There will have to an inquest," said Reuben. "If you have the details of her solicitor, let them know straight away, so that they get her affairs in order. Is there anything I can do for you?" Mitch declined his offer but felt he should know. Thanking him and repeating how shocked and sorry he was at the news, Reuben put the phone down. For some reason he also felt upset, bearing in mind he had only met them yesterday; she had looked so well. His job put him in close contact with death and its repercussions more so than that of any other profession, bar the military, but it was still an unpleasant experience. A dark feeling enveloped him, and he shuddered. *Pull yourself together,* he thought. Standing up, he walked over to the radio terminal took out a fresh battery and turned his handset on. A quick shout out to the operator booked him on and confirmed there was nothing for him.

"Roger that; I will be conducting vehicle checks this morning," was his reply.

Having dressed ready for patrol, Reuben descended the stairs and opened the small room under the stairs, where all the cleaning products were, and filled a bucket with bottles, rags and assorted sprays.

As he left the station, he placed a wedge under the heavy

door, so that he could hear if the phone rang, and filled the bucket with freezing water from the exterior wall tap.

The station used to have two cars, one of which was a new Land Rover Freelander, whose engine blew after about three weeks, and was never replaced.

He took his time enjoying the early morning sunshine, and casual conversations with the pedestrians who bothered to pass the time of day with him, and it was about an hour before he had finished the exterior.

Once he had returned the cleaning equipment, and ditched the dirty water in the drain, he returned to the car and opened the boot. Holding the boot open he studied the box lying between the three traffic cones and road closure signs. *Was it a stupid, and potentially sackable thing that he was doing, or was it just a whim, which may wear off?* Closing the boot lid, he locked the car, and went back to the room under the stairs and turned the light on. He knew what he was looking for and quickly found the large black bin bags and black packing tape.

Leaving the station to get into the car he called up on the radio asking if there was anything for him.

"Negative for the Seaton area, over," was the reply.

"In that case code 8 paperwork and file preparation please." This meant that he would not be bothered unless in an emergency. Reuben had a plan, bought together because of a chance meeting and memories of a life and a career long since gone, madness pure madness, but he did not care.

Twenty minutes later the gleaming patrol car pulled into the carpark at the entrance to the start of the bridle path in Musberry. It ran along the river and was a favourite spot for a lunch break for Reuben and his opposite number in Axminster. There was one way in and one way out, and he knew the area well, and backed the car in with ease.

Taking the small spade from the boot, which was normally used at the scene of road traffic collisions, or removal of animal carcasses from the road, he strode off onto the pathway, with the River Axe to his right. When in the Royal Marines, he had been an instructor and was an expert in many military subjects, one of which was map reading. Reuben knew that for every hundred metres on even ground, he would take on average one hundred and ten paces. The idea behind this is that when trying to navigate either in the dark or inclement weather, if your bearing were correct, you could arrive at a location with almost deadly accuracy. Reuben was counting to himself, as he walked, eighty, eighty-one, eighty-two. Looking up and beyond him he could see a tall old oak tree and decided to aim to stop beside it. At one hundred and fifteen paces, the tree was beside him and, turning left, he entered the thicket and keeping the tree to his left continued for another twenty paces, in a straight line, emerging into a small but overhung clearing. Dropping the spade he unhooked his belt and radio and placed to his rear. The area was a haven for wildlife, and the birds had got use to the noise he had made walking through the undergrowth and were chirping away merrily. Pausing with his hands on his waist, he listened for anything untoward, dog walkers, anglers, cyclists. There was nothing. *Good*, he thought.

The ground was moist and easy to dig, taking about twenty minutes to excavate a small narrow trench. Standing up he allowed himself a small grin. Placing the shovel on the ground he put his belt on and walked back to the car. Unlocking it he took out the duct tape and roll of bin liners. Opening two of the bags, he slipped them over each end of the slim box and stood it up against the side of the car, and stuffed the rest of the bags and tape, into his high visibility vest. As he was about to lift the concealed box, he felt that someone was watching, and slowly but deliberately straightened, and closed the boot. Turning he saw an elderly woman walking towards him, with an excitable terrier, on a lead to her front.

Reuben walked towards her.

"Good morning my love, I don't suppose you've seen a couple of lads with fishing rods on your travels, have you?"

The lady reeled the dog in and approached Reuben.

"No, I'm sorry, I have only just come out; are they in trouble?"

Reuben thought quickly and explained that their parents were concerned, and they should return home; he was not sure where they were but was just having a quick look.

"If I see them I will tell them; have a good day," said the lady, who then turned and called to her dog. "Come on Tiff, leave the officer to his business."

Reuben thanked her and watched as the women walked back in the direction she had just come from, pulled faster than she would have wanted by the energetic little mutt. Deciding to wait for a while, he watched the lady as she disappeared, until he could not hear anything. Sweating from the digging, and secreted black plastic bags, he let out a long sigh, and retraced his steps into the undergrowth, with his secret under his right arm.

He plonked himself beside the oblong hole, and swung his legs into it, sitting on the dry earth he had removed, and removing the bags and tape, placing them at his feet.

It took him about ten minutes to cover and tape the rifle and box, which now also contained the box of ammunition. He reckoned that he used about eighteen bags and all the tape, to ensure it was waterproof. Ideally, he would have buried a plastic barrel or container, as the IRA had done during the Troubles in Northern Ireland to hide their explosives and weapons, methods he was skilled at. However, time was not on his side. Laying the box down in the gaping hole, he stood up and started back filling the earth, until the cache had been totally covered.

Happy with the result, he shuffled leaves and loose soil over it with his feet, picked up the shovel and returned to the car, careful to walk in the same footsteps he had made entering earlier. This method was known as track discipline, and was a method used in the military to negate disturbance of plants and soil and disguise the number of persons who had used it.

When Reuben looked back at the route in, he was pleased. Give it a couple of days and let the fauna grow back and you would never know; even now, the untrained eye would not know that someone had walked that route. All skills that he had kept and relished.

Sitting in the car, Reuben questioned why he was doing what he was doing. It was the thought of the weapon being sent to an anonymous civilian worker at Headquarters, who would simply run it through the machine, which would smash, and cut it to pieces, with all the other weapons obtained through the amnesty. This rifle had history, precision, and was a weapon of distance death, as they called it on his sniper course. He recalled the motto, that they had unofficially adopted for T-shirts: *Don't Run You Will Only Die Tired*. It had raised eyebrows, and laughter when first suggested, but they were never openly worn, it was always as an undergarment, on the course.

Reuben thought of the all the time Yvonne's husband had used and cleaned the rifle, time after time, and the people it had sent on their way. Reuben felt that he owed it to him, and his memory, even if it stayed in that dark cold hole forever. His guilty secret.

Exiting the bridle path, and now in the car, he decided not to visit Mitch, and the now empty and lonely house. He went straight back to the nick, and assaulted the biscuit jar, and reams of paperwork that needed seeing to.

CHAPTER SEVENTEEN

Reuben woke with a start and sat upright; he looked around in the dark. His heart was racing, and he was soaked in sweat. Sarah was sleeping beside him. He had gone to bed late again. His head was racing and full of guilt. He had never ever crossed the line, as a police officer and had always been a law-abiding person with high moral values. What was he doing, it was sackable, pension, family, reputation, media, the lot would all come crashing down, but he had no answers. Sarah always slept well, and an earthquake would not wake her, lucky sod. Lying back down, he glanced at his watch: 0400hrs. He knew that he would not go back to sleep, although he wanted to badly.

He remembered the dream, a bad dream. Yvonne was with her husband, and it must have been during the Second World War. They were in a farmhouse, on the Austrian-German border, and her husband had volunteered to fight a rear-guard action, against the allies, as they swept through the Alps. Both were gravely wounded, and she was helping her husband load his rifle, as he picked off the approaching Americans. It felt real, and Reuben felt like he was above them watching helplessly, calling out for them to surrender, to survive, to live on, but it was in vain, and he felt sad. He was helpless and did not want to watch this. It was at this point he had woken. It is almost as they were trying to tell him that everything would be okay, that he should forget his doubts, and feel better in himself, leave the guilt behind.

Turning to Sarah, he knew he was in a good place; he loved

Sarah and the kids and was looking forward to applying for the traffic department, with a view to getting on to the Elite Armed Response Vehicles. The road he had to take was hard, demanding, and the attrition rate was high, but he was determined, and committed. Closing his eyes, his thoughts drifted to the future, and what might be, and he smiled.

CHAPTER EIGHTEEN

DECEMBER 2004

The whole team had felt the pressure of the incident in Wadebridge. Phil had made a point of getting them all together when they had returned to Exeter on the day of the job.

Once they had cleaned and stashed all their kit, he called a meeting in the small but soundproofed armoury, in the car park. They were all present when Phil entered with a tray of steaming coffee cups, and an unopened packet of Jammy Dodgers, the team's favourite and passed the tray to Simon, who offered the tray around. Phil closed the door and turned to them all.

"Guys, I just wanted to say thank you for a great professional job, it was a bad one, but both me and the bosses wanted you to know. They are chuffed to bits." Phil went on to say that he was due to attend both an update and debrief later that day, despite it being a day off for them all. One of the downsides of being a skipper. He went on to say that upon their return from rest days in two days' time, they would be used in their search team roles on the Wadebridge job and were likely to be on it for months. Their team's primary role was always the Force's response to any firearms job, but their training, which was continuous, was also in searching, and public order, the latter being at an extremely high level. Often the searching was monotonous, and tedious although necessary, in all weathers and in any location. They were trained to use every gardening implement you could imagine up to and including chainsaws, cherry pickers, and other mechanical pieces of equipment.

The upcoming two days off would be a welcome break, before the undoubted challenging work yet to come. Phil left them without drinking the coffee he had made; he had looked tired Reuben had thought.

"Well, it will be watch on, stop on for the next couple of months then, stacks of overtime and decent food," said Jason.

"Wonder if they'll send the food wagon down or let us eat locally," replied Brian.

That was the humour of the team, black though it was, it helped in masking people's true feelings, which would appear eventually some time down the line.

"Me and Simon are up for a few beers at the Barn Owl, when were done here, if anyone's up for it," piped Rick.

Lucky that they were single, and the others declined, with an urgency to get back to their loved ones. Eventually after several phone calls to partners, and family it was confirmed that it would only be the two of them to go to the pub, much to the jealousy of some of the others, who had been told to get home.

Reuben did not feel in the mood for a drink, and, was looking forward to getting home, to give Sarah and the kids a big hug, and settle into a chilled-out couple of days, as the weather forecast was good again. A chance to get stuck into the garden and do some of the unimportant things that needed doing around the house, but which had been delayed thanks to the demands of work.

As expected, the days shot by, and Reuben was awoken by the alarm beside the bed again, muscle memory and the light sleeping meant he could cancel the ringing almost as soon as it started. Sarah lying beside him, stirred a little, but turned over away from him, and snuggled even deeper into the duvet. It was five o'clock, and in Sarah's mind she and the family were in Spain beside a warm beach, without a care in the world, and would probably remain there for another hour or so, before she too had to rise, and shake a leg.

Unusually Reuben had yearned for a savoury start to the day and gulped down the two slices of granary toast which had a liberal covering of Marmite on, before leaving the house, to go to the garage, coffee in hand. Walking in through the side door, he turned the light on and placed the hot drink on the saddle of his Honda. It was going to a continuing warm week, so he reached up and unhooked his paddock jacket, deciding against the full leather set. The coffee begged to be gulped down, which he did gladly, then placed the empty mug to one side and put on his helmet.

The journey was sedate and leisurely; traffic was light, and he felt good, arriving at work within fifteen minutes.

All the team, as normal were seated with at least ten minutes, before start time, mugs in hand laughing and musing at the last two days, which all agreed had simply disappeared. Phil entered and sat down, with the assortment of maps and pens, which was to be taken down to Wadebridge.

There was an unusually quiet atmosphere that descended upon them as Phil had sat down, it was not because of anything, more of a need to know what they were going to do.

"Reuben, can you clear the table, and get the coffees away from the map?"

Each team member removed their cups, and automatically reached for something to weight the map down, as Phil laid it out. He had been to the Headquarters map room, and prioritised an order for them, as usually it would need an order number and countless signatures, placing it in an ever-extending queue. Laid before them was a detailed enlarged ordinance survey map which centred on the small group of buildings, that they had entered, only two days earlier. The large map extended to over seven thousand metres from the buildings, and the reprographic department had superimposed several continuous thin-lined circles, expanding out from a midway point on the farm buildings, each circle accurately represented two hundred metres.

Phil leant over the map and held an extended pointer.

"Okay guys, the plot is here," and placed the pointer on the farm shop. "We will conduct searches, outside of the buildings after we have sectorised the areas. We will not search the buildings, or even enter them of the immediate grounds to negate cross contamination."

Everyone nodded in agreement. Phil explained that Plymouth's team would spend the next three days, more if required, within the plot, to retrieve and preserve evidence.

"The weather for the next two weeks is on our side, and the days will be twelve-hour days, with plenty of scope for overtime if needed. The Senior Officer in charge is right on it, and the intelligence cell is already turning up good leads, he wants meticulous and thorough searches lads."

The team were elated when they were informed that their food would be provided by the local pub, The Tally Ho, with an individual allowance of ten pounds per person

The briefing took about an hour, and each knew what was needed. Leaving the room, they got into their black search overalls, and loaded the two vehicles from the search store. This included a couple of hedge trimmers, bill hooks, and an assortment of rakes, prodders, and marker flags. Having loaded up the vehicles they began the first of what was to be many trips up and down the A38 to Wadebridge.

The task was laborious and vast, with the team split into pairs. For the first week, they concentrated on house-to-house enquiries, on every specific property, within the expanding search area, including derelict buildings. Intelligence that came into the Operation Headquarters in Padstowe would be manually entered into the major incident computer, which was operated by specially trained in putters. This in turn produced what is known as actions, and each had a unique reference number. Actions were issued and given to individual officers, to conduct the necessary enquiry and return them completed.

As the days passed, the search circle around the area increased. Hedgerows were cut down; drains were examined; rivers were waded in, and burrows were crawled into. The feedback from briefings had confirmed the two women's identities, and the fact they had been shot to death. Although it was not exactly sure of the motive, the team at Padstowe were still pursuing the motive as being financial. The odd thing is, neither of the vehicles had been found, either by visual sighting or the nationwide number plate recognition readers up and down the main arterial routes. This would suggest that the plates had been changed, or that they had been destroyed or hidden somewhere.

After over a week of endless searching, the pairing of search teams changed and Reuben was paired with Simon for the next five days. It was Monday morning, and they had all just arrived at the drop-off point, which just happened to be at the very pub they were eating at every day. Phil was in a good mood but had to attend a meeting at Padstowe, leaving John in charge, with clear instructions and a pile of actions. All teams would set off from the pub, returning at midday for wash-up and early lunch, before going back out in the afternoon.

"Reuben, if you walk out with Simon, and call at an address first, it's action C49, about something a local has to say, and give me a shout when you are squared away." Taking the action from him, Simon walked over to Reuben, opening the folder as he did. A quick glance, and they looked at the map that Reuben held. His stumpy finger ran up the side of the map sprawled out on the floor in front of them, and found the first set of numbers, the Eastings, while his other finger ran along the bottom for the second set, the Northings. The he traced the invisible two lines where they met at a small group of buildings on the scaled map called Mint Farm. He estimated that it was about 1500 metres, and easy to get to; the man to ask for was Rod Kellick.

Some of the pairs left in vehicles, weighed down with gardening equipment and flasks of hot water. Simon and Reuben left with their clipboards and generic questionnaires, walking out of the pub's car park and turning right. As they did so, their colleagues' vehicles passed in quick succession, each with a torrent of abuse being hurled at the pair. As they passed both raised a single digit in reply and laughed.

Although time was passing slowly for all the team, they knew that what they were doing was a necessary evil, and these apparently mundane tasks had a habit of turning up things that could change things dramatically. The whole team had been stood down from anything but the most urgent Firearms job, due to the hours that they all worked, whilst carrying firearms. They were conscious of this but knew the other teams were as good in that role, and while the weather was as gorgeous as it had been, and the dinners that had been supplied were first class, it was not so bad really.

As they walked, Reuben looked at Simon.

"Penny for your thoughts, mate."

Simon looked up and smiled.

"Oh nothing really, mate, just can't fathom this job out really, the violence; it's just like whoever did it enjoyed it, if you know what I mean." He asked Reuben if he had read the brief on the mother and daughter victims, and their life stories which bought them from London down to Bodmin Moor. Reuben said he had.

"I know what you mean Simon, it's a weird one for sure, but well get the fuckers, of that I am certain, we just need a break." The lads reached the farm in a leisurely twenty minutes, and as they approached the old wooden gates, which were open, a black-and-white collie with piercing blue eyes ran to greet them, tail wagging furiously. Reuben and Simon froze as the energetic bedraggled dog bounded towards them barking.

"Fletch!" a voice shouted, and the dog stopped in its tracks and lay down at the feet of the two lads. The high Devon bank hid the figure which had shouted, but they could hear the footsteps coming towards the entrance. The dog leapt up and ran back from where it had come. The figure of a tall man appeared from around the gate post to their left.

"Mr Kellick, Rod Kellick? We're police and would like to have a chat if that's possible," shouted Simon, waving the folder in the air.

"Sorry about that gents, its Fletch, he's all wind, and wouldn't hurt a fly." Rod greeted the two with a handshake that would crush a bar of soap. "Please come in, cup of tea, or something stronger boys?"

Reuben looked at Simon and grinned. "Something cold and non-alcoholic would be lovely," Simon said, nodding, and they all went in through the gates and entered the yard.

The farm was obviously kept in good order and Simon asked what he farmed.

"Well, prior to foot-and-mouth, it was a large Friesian dairy herd, but all were destroyed, all three hundred in one afternoon, and burnt two days later."

Both Simon and Reuben had policed the foot-and-mouth episode, for many weeks, and knew of the awful scenes and slaughter that took place.

"I reckon it was the most unpleasant things I have ever policed or witnessed," said Reuben.

"We were all down around this way then," added Simon. Rod cleared his throat. "Would you believe I now work as a, how can I say, agency type farmer."

The two officers looked puzzled. "That means I use all my equipment to assist others, they hire me, almost like subcontract work, I work the hours I want to on a day rate, with no stress," he smiled, and it appeared that he liked what he was doing. "Sometimes I just hire my stuff out, equipment and the like."

Rod directed them to the yard which was immaculate, and a long wooden table with benches.

"Sit yourselves down, and I'll get the drinks and join you."

Sitting down, they took off their baseball caps, and laid the paperwork out in front of them, and Rod disappeared out of sight.

As they were both soaking up the warmth of the sun, Rod reappeared with a tray of drinks, and his ever-eager dog walking beside him. Sitting at the table he passed the two drinks across and encouraged the dog to greet the two officers. The dog needed no encouragement and lapped up the attention he got from both.

Simon read from the typed action, as he made a note of the time and date.

"Mr Kellick—may we call you Rod?"

The farmer nodded, and raised his glass and took a long swig.

"Rod, you rang the incident room yesterday and left a message saying you had located something which may be connected to the murders."

Rod placed the glass down and stood up. "Yep, I hope I'm not wasting your time; I'll go and fetch it." As he walked away and entered the house, Reuben looked at Simon, with a puzzled expression, and cocked his head to one side. Both were intrigued as to what he was going to bring out. At their feet, the dog was oblivious to everything and was fast asleep, not stirring even when his master went into the farmhouse. Rod appeared from the front door and appeared to be carrying something which was wrapped in a piece of old hessian. "I think this may be of interest to you," Rod said as he offered the hidden item over and sat down. Reuben laid it on the table and opened the loose wrapping. At first, there was an uncomfortable silence as both officers looked at what had been revealed. In front of them were a set of shotgun barrels, which had been cut down, about eighteen inches long. Reuben moved closer to have a better look, whilst reaching into his trouser pocket, bringing out a pair of blue rubber gloves.

"Rod where and how did you find these?"

Simon made his apologies and left the table to make a phone call to the incident room at Padstowe. Rod explained that he had been asked to use his tractor, and hedge trimmer on a lane just outside of Wadebridge, a minor road, but one which was well known to locals and circumnavigated the main route into the busy town. As a matter of course, he would always walk the route, in stages, to scout the hedgerows for anything obvious, such as metal objects or large stones and rocks, before cutting started. He had seen the barrels in a thicket almost immediately.

"If I arranged it, could you show us exactly where?" Reuben asked and produced a photocopied map which was within many creased paper notes and wrappers and smoothed it out on the table. Rod took out his glasses and scrutinised the map before him. He recognised the locations and drew his finger along a road stopping at the point he thought was the location where he had found the barrels. Reuben raised the creased paper and asked if, he was sure.

Rod nodded excitedly.

"Simon, it's at grid 0945 1550." Simon raised a thumb and relayed the coordinates to the voice on the other end of the phone.

"Rod has anyone else touched these since you found them?" Rod explained that he had thought about the possibility they were of interest and had picked them up with the hessian, which had been in the tractor, and put them safely in the cab. Simon joined Reuben and sat down with a medium-sized paper exhibits bag. Reuben folded the hessian and carefully wrapped the barrels. After Simon had completed the exhibit label with all the relevant details, the barrels were placed in the bag.

"Rod, can we go now, as I am conscious there may be other things that may be of interest to the enquiry where you found these."

The farmer stood up and nodded.

"No worries."

The journey seemed to take only a matter of several minutes, and Reuben stopped the car at the start of the road, about fifty metres away from the exact spot. Simon got out and took a roll of blue-and-white scene tape from the boot, spreading it across the road behind the car. Returning to the boot he also removed a couple of traffic cones, to also enforce the area was a scene of interest to the police. Rod and Reuben joined Simon, and together they walked the short distance, with the two policeman eagerly looking at the hedgerow as they went. It was a narrow road, with barely space for two cars to pass each other, only made easier with the occasional passing space in the Devon banks.

Rod slowed and faced the hedge, looking left and right. To his feet there was a granite rock, which looked out of place.

"I put that there just to remind me," said Rod. Simon and Reuben unfurled the roll of tape, placing a strip of it on branches above the stone. Rod explained that the barrels appeared to have been placed or thrown, as they were in the top of the hedgerow, and not buried further down.

Simon's phone rang, and he answered, passing it to Reuben, it was Phil.

"Cracking result mate; what's the update mate," said the voice.

"We have sealed the entrance to the road from the east, and Rod has kindly left a marker for us, which we have also taped."

Reuben smiled at Rod as he said this, and Rod felt chuffed knowing he had done the right thing in a short space of time, another search team had been dispatched, to ensure there was no contamination of evidence and Phil had arranged for a CID officer to go to Rod's farm to obtain a statement. The two officers were to return with the barrels to the incident room in Wadebridge.

The three waited until the search team arrived, as the CID officer also arrived to collect Rod.

"Do you think this is connected to the murders?" asked the inquisitive farmer.

Simon paused. "I am not a betting man, Rod, but I think you'd be a fool not to put good money on the odds," and smiled. Shaking hands warmly the three split up, with Rod walking down to the plain clothes officer who had walked toward them from her car, at the other end of the road, and the two happy officers returning to their car.

As they parked outside of Wadebridge, there was a small welcoming party to greet them. Phil was at the front with the senior investigating officer and Bob Crook, the Scenes of Crime boss from Exeter, clipboard in hand. Simon took the paper bag out of the boot and Reuben locked the car. Exchanging pleasantries, they all entered the station and went to the incident room.

"If we go into the exhibits room, lads, I've got a table ready," exclaimed an excited Bob. Taking the bag from Simon, Bob signed the label which was attached, ensuring continuity, and noted the time, telling Simon, "Many a job had been lost in court due to the gap in continuity of exhibits."

Reuben and Simon left a short time after, having completed their statements, driving back to Exeter, leaving Phil and the excited investigators behind to decide their next course of action.

Examination of the barrels was prioritised, and involved minute investigation, swabs being taken and a blue light motorcycle blast to the labs at Chepstow for an urgent test on a possible DNA discovery. Twelve hours later, the DNA results were in, and the very same motorcycle rider delivered the physical confirmation to Wadebridge.

The technicians at Chepstow had already rung the Incident room to verbally inform them of the two DNA matches which had been recovered from the barrels. Both matches were beyond doubt and shocked the examining detectives.

CHAPTER NINETEEN

The incident commander had called the team together, as well as the search team sergeants, local officers and firearms skippers Phil and Simon at 2100hrs the next night.

The atmosphere was electric. Each team member eagerly took their seats, blue notebooks to hand awaiting the enquiry's breaking news. The incident commander entered the room with the intel sergeant and unknown female police officer, who was there to presumably take notes.

"Ladies and gentlemen, thank you for being here, at this late hour. I know you have all worked long hours and days, but the information I have to hand is about to launch the enquiry forward into a previously unknown direction. We are certain that the barrels are part of at least one of the guns used on our victims in this enquiry."

There was an audible gasp and shuffling in seats, at the anticipation of what was to come.

"We submitted DNA of both victims at the same time and have received two positive DNA matches." Turning the pages on the desk in front of him, he reached into a pocket and retrieved his glasses which he put on and adjusted before continuing. "There is blood DNA from one of the victims, Tilly Light, and sweat DNA from a male identified as Thomas Burns." The room was eerily silent, and there were glances from one to the other, and puzzled expressions. No one had heard of anyone called Thomas Burns, or no one could remember anyone with that name anyway. Burns is a well-known habitual traveller from the area of Southeast London, with a network of unsavoury individuals within the criminal fraternity. He is one of a twin with his brother being called Michael Burns.

They went on to talk in depth about the evil Burns Twins but were at a loss to link them to the small shop in sleepy Cornwall.

The Intelligence Sergeant, Dan Bilk, an old-school guy, near retirement, with links to all the other forces and a career of making and keeping valuable contacts spoke.

"I have been in touch with the Met, and they tell me that their most recent intel is that the Burns boys are in our neck of the woods, and have been visitors here, on and off for a number of months. They have been using local crims and their knowledge to drive them around, probably doing burglaries." The weary looking sergeant said that there were several outstanding high-value burglaries that had occurred at substantial dwellings or business premises, all of which had been unoccupied at the time of the offences. In all of them one thing in common was entry via smashed windows, and untidy searches.

"We are trying to house Thomas Burns as we speak. The Met have made enquiries up there and the feeling is they are here somewhere."

The incident commander removed his glasses and addressed the audience, slowly and deliberately.

"This information is classified, and we are actively pursuing lines of enquiries to find this individual. I have a feeling that when we do, and we will, we will also find his brother, Michael." The door behind the briefing team opened and a plain-clothes detective leant in extending his arm towards the speakers.

"Excuse me, boss, you need to see this, sorry."

The superintendent stood up and took the note, reading from

it, as the interrupting constable awaited a response.

"Thank you, Tim."

The door closed, and the young officer disappeared. The operation commander sat down, and quickly scribbled into his notes, then looked up scanning his audience.

"Hot off the press, information received via Crime Stoppers, The Burns lads are staying at a remote farmhouse cottage, near Haytor, on Dartmoor just outside of Bovey Tracey. Surveillance Teams as we speak are on scene to confirm."

He stood up and placed his hands on his waist, and exhaled loudly, nodding his head from side to side.

"Phil, Simon, get your teams together; I will get Firearms Authority. Once the intel is confirmed, I want these fuckers, cuffed, and stuffed, do we understand each other?"

Both officers stood in unison, and left the room, tapping into the phones as they marched down the corridors.

Both teams had been warned off before and were awaiting an update, sat in their vans, in the rear yard. The phone calls from the two sergeants began the rehearsed drills of kitting up and getting ready to deploy.

As both skippers entered the back yard, the shout went up and both teams grouped together in the area between the two vans which had been backed closer together. The interior lights gave excellent light for any night-time brief.

Phil addressed both teams with Simon stood by his side, phone in hand, with all the info they had to hand.

He could sense the excitement building as he continued, all their eyes burning into his soaking up the information, hanging on every word.

As soon as he had finished, all he said was, "Guys, let's get to it," to start a flurry of activity and fetching of kit and equipment. Phil and Simon had already dressed, and were ready, with enough time to have been individually briefed and confirmed the authority to deploy with Firearms, as it was a pre-planned job.

CHAPTER TWENTY

The police helicopter, call sign Oscar 99, had overflown the plot, at its maximum operating height, and taken infrared images, not ideal but they had to act, and act now.

The images confirmed that there were several vehicles at the location, two showing heat sources, indicating the engines had been running recently.

There were two covert rural surveillance officers at the location conducting close target reconnaissance, as they were examining the images, who were live feeding information to the incident room, who in turn relayed it to the firearms teams.

Two pairs of officers in the sniper teams had deployed from the offices in North Devon, to obtain and dominate the high ground, otherwise known as over watch.

Phil and Simon would move the teams forward to the car park of a licenced hotel north of Bovey Tracey, and hold until the surveillance guys, and snipers had both settled. It was about ten minutes travelling time between the locations and was hidden from view. On this occasion they would only take the two Mercedes Sprinter vans, leaving the Range Rovers and drivers at the station.

As the guys were getting all the kit and weapons, other resources began to gather, in and around Bovey Tracey. These included ambulance and fire brigade staff and vehicles, police negotiators, two Firearms dogs and their handlers.

The helicopter had returned to Exeter, to refuel, and would

remain there until just before the strike was given to hover above the teams, using its thermal imagery and bright night sun light, should it be needed.

Information continued to bombard the Firearms teams, via the incident room, which seemed to be mostly for the skippers. An unconscious filter in the brain sifts through all the information allowing an individual to continue with the task in hand, and concentrate on it, only pausing when it pertained to either him or the task in hand.

The two Sprinter vans, loaded and straining under the weight, exited the rear of Wadebridge Station, with Phil's van driven by Mick, closely followed by Simon, his driver Jo and the Plymouth lads. The sat navs indicated it would take about one and a half hours if driven within the speed limits. They would be able to make valuable time when they reach the A38 in about nine miles, and then onwards to the edge of Dartmoor and the rendezvous at the Edge Moor Hotel.

As they joined the A38 at the Dobwalls roundabout they settled into a steady pace. Phil turned to the rear and looked at the team. All were quiet, and some had their eyes closed. The chatter on the radio had died down, and he had received as much of the information that he had wanted in the time given. There would be more at the car park, where they would meet with other officers, and consult directly with the teams on the ground. His hand dropped to the holster on his right thigh, where the Glock pistol was housed. He had already loaded one magazine on to it and chambered a round. The good thing about a Glock pistol is that there is not a physical safety catch; it can only be fired if held correctly and the trigger is pulled. The idea behind this is to minimise accidental discharges and negates the weapon firing if it is dropped. All the team's weapons had lighting systems attached. The pistols had a small but intensely bright one attached to the underside of the barrel and is turned on or off by the firer easily with a finger, designed so that it does not alter a firing position when levelling the sights at a target.

Slipping the locking strap off, Phil withdrew the weapon slightly and turned the light on briefly. As he did, the strong beam hit the floor of the van, immediately burning into his thigh, which he felt. Turning the light off, he housed the weapon and locked it into place with the strap. The raid would begin in the early hours and the light was paramount. Turning to his right he called over to the packed passenger compartment.

"Just make sure all your light sources, are working, if you need fresh Duracells, they are in the plastic box under the table." Turning to face the front again he was conscious of weapons being drawn and momentary flashes of light behind him and smiled.

It seemed like only half an hour before both vehicles left the main A38, at Drum Bridges roundabout slip road, signposted Bovey Tracey, but had taken the full ninety minutes with the blue strobes piercing the blackness, and traffic relatively light. Both vehicles passed through the sets of red traffic lights, taking the second turning on to Bovey straits, with ease. They were about seven to ten minutes until the Edge Moor Hotel, and Phil radioed Simon, and his team who were stuck to them like glue, behind him.

As they reached the end of the strait, both vehicles stopped the blue lights, and silently turned left on the road that led to their destination.

Approaching the entrance, on the right, there was a hive of activity and high visibility jackets running around like busy little bugs. As they turned onto the gravelly drive, the hotel was in darkness, and the car park to the left had only a couple of private vehicles.

Both vans slowly drove to the rear of the car park and parked having reversed in against the trees.

Phil joined Simon, and the vans spewed out the black-clad officers. The sight of two full teams kitted up was still something to impress. Each member had a specialism, from explosive entry specialists to snipers, to combat medics; the latter being identified by the green cross patch on their shoulders and compact backpack.

Reuben was one of the team's snipers and the explosives expert. He had attended the Royal Military College of Science in Shrivenham on the Oxfordshire-Wiltshire border after an internal advert was posted within the authorised Firearms Departments throughout the Force looking for volunteers. Together with twelve other officers from around the country, and Northern Ireland, they had trained in a Welsh Quarry, and purpose-built firearms range, near Betws-y-Coed. Their chief instructor had been a Special Forces Explosives Operator, who was retired and looked after the super rich on their super yachts in the Caribbean. Reuben had left the course with the knowledge and know-how, that ensured that the teams would be able to access any entry point, whether it be a vehicle, dwelling or vessel.

Today the sniper rifle was not needed as teams had already been deployed and were relaying constant updates and live feeds back to the incident room, and troops on the ground. The two sergeants approached the group.

"Guys just kit check and chill; the job is defo a go," said Phil, as he turned and they entered the command post van, which was stuck right into the corner the car park. Tall telescopic lights were positioned at its side, turning dark into day.

With the two sergeants there were four complete four-man teams. All would be needed before the sun rose.

After about fifteen minutes, the two skippers climbed out of the van and strode purposefully towards the assembled teams. Nudges and taps on shoulders alerted busy individuals as they readied themselves.

The teams formed up in their small groups in front of Phil and Simon and prepared for the update. The information was delivered by them, almost as if it were rehearsed. Slow paced, deliberate, correct, and repeated where necessary. The information, which had been confirmed by several sources, placed the two brothers at the address with an as yet unknown number of associates. This was because of constant observations since deployment from the two pairs of sniper teams. The observations had placed all the people in one building, the main farmhouse. This made the execution of entry easier, but the unknown number of persons in total was an issue. It had been decided that rather than surround, and instigate communication via a negotiator, a rapid entry using stun grenades was to be used. The primary thinking for this was to preserve any evidence, followed by the possibility of weapons on the persons in the house.

Each team member already had four flash-bang stun grenades on their person. Each grenade had a two-second delay and was made up of nine small charges accompanied by instantaneous blinding flashes. Unless the body of the grenade struck you, they would not physically harm you. They would temporarily make you unable to function and were an extremely effective method to use upon entry. Total confusion and massive interruption of all the senses. The teams had practised with these and trusted them implicitly.

The sound of footsteps on the gravel made them look up. It was their Firearms boss, Chief Inspector Ged Oldham. Ged was old school, and a Firearms Officer of many years, and had been a transferee from the West Mids. Now he had seen it all and got the T-shirt. He managed all the training and selection, and most importantly was the go-to man for finance and kit. Although he was not authorised to carry firearms now, he was a trusted and revered man, and when he spoke people listened. No one had a bad word to say about him. As he approached the group, everyone stood up straight, and made room for him to join them.

"Morning lads, game's on now," he said, as he looked around, and focused on the two skippers. "Are you sure you've got everything you need?" They nodded, and Ged smiled. "Those nine bangs are forty-five quid a pop, make sure you use the lot." The gathered audience burst into nervous laughter. Ged cleared his throat and waited until the laughter had subsided. Then he spoke with authority and sincerity.

"This morning you will put into practice everything you have trained for. All these years gents, all down to days like this. Concentrate, look after yourselves and your buddies, see you back here for tea and biscuits later!" He then warmly and firmly shook every team member's hand, turned, and returned to the van. He would be the advisor and the last voice they heard before they entered and the first one on completion, apart from other team members.

Simon then clapped his gloved hands together twice.

"Load up, and we move off in five."

As the teams took their places, the drivers started the cold engines and put the heaters on to clear the misty interiors. Windows were wound down a little to let the air circulate, and the doors were closed. The blacked-out windows disguised the fact that these were not normal patrol vans which was handy when trying to hide the identity of its cargo.

Each vehicle was designed to be self-sufficient and fit for purpose. This meant it had to be able to carry the teams with all their kit, which is a lot due to their dual roles, and different responsibilities. The flasks were always full of hot water and there was a plentiful supply of assorted biscuits.

Phil's van, closely followed by Simon's team, pulled out of the car park and turned right and started the climb up towards Haytor, and the farmhouse. They took the signposted fork in the road, passing Ulla combe Farm, which had a superb restaurant, and butchery, a hidden gem, often enjoyed by the teams on down days.

The windy road took them higher and higher onto the moor, and into the inevitable mist, which appeared to swallow the vehicles like a huge demon. The moor was notorious for sudden and unexpected weather changes at short notice, often with little or no notice. The Royal Marines amongst the two teams had hundreds of hours' experience amongst them of walking on the moor, and they were used to the clag and mist.

The vehicles slowed, and as if they were linked turned in unison to the lower car park, situated below and to the left of the Tor.

The buildings were to be accessed on foot, so each vehicle turned its lights off and parked up side by side. All four teams gathered at the rear doors.

"Guys, if you get in file now, my team Alpha first, followed by Bravo, and the Plymouth lads." Phil's voice was a clear whisper. Silently the teams shuffled positions and took their places. Phil watched as without a word; the teams formed a single line. Simon headed team three, the Plymouth boys. A noise to the left caught Phil's attention, and he raised a clenched fist and motioned for the team to crouch. As they did, a figure appeared from the darkness. It had been hard to see him, as he was one of the North Devon sniper team members whom Phil recognised as Steve, another ex-Royal Marine, and somewhat of a natural expert at stalking and long shots. He was carrying his Accuracy International sniper rifle at his side in his right hand. His body shape had been disrupted with the ghillie suit, a must for all snipers and made to suit the individual. He had removed his face veil, which revealed tactical face paint, with a glistening of sweat. Kneeling beside Phil, he waved to Simon, to join him.

"Nice to see you guys. It's freezing out on the ground." Laying the weapon down he continued, whilst quietly rubbing his gloved hands together. "There's no change to what you have been told. We have housed all the people in the main building, and we have positively identified both Subject one and Subject two, the Burns lads."

Steve confirmed the route in and suggested it would take no more than eight or nine minutes to reach the Lay Up Point or LUP, from which the lads would await the strike command.

"I will lead you in, and from the LUP I will dog leg and take up my post. Once that's done, I shall tell Silver, and wait for your move—oh and one other thing, we have not seen any weapons, we reckon on maybe three other persons so in total five baddies." Steve smiled, and both skippers shook his extended hand. Picking up his weapon he took his place at the head of the lengthy line. A succession of gentle squeezes on each shoulder continued up the line until Phil squeezed the sniper's shoulder. A silent and distinctive signal telling the lead man that everyone was ready to go. Phil keyed his send button, and everyone's headset crackled.

"Silver from Total One Alpha and Bravo, and Total Two

Alpha and Bravo, moving to LUP, over."

The Silver Commander down below in the car park quickly replied.

"Roger, I have control." This single comment told everyone that the teams were committed, and until such point that it changed, the Silver Commander still had control of the teams and what they did.

Slowly and deliberately, the line moved off. Each team member had extended an arm and had grabbed the person in front, on their shoulder. This was to keep the team together and let each person know that all were moving as one. The snake of officers disappeared into the darkness of the trees and bushes, one by one, until the car park was empty.

The radio was quiet, and they moved up the track.

"No change, no change," the radio echoed. One of the teams who were watching the building was the conduit for anything that happened. He or She was the 'eyeball'. The eyeball was informing everyone that there had been no change since the last transmission almost ten minutes previously. This confirmed that the targets were still in the main building.

As the line reached the fork in the track, Steve raised his fist, and the teams knelt. Turning to Phil he patted his shoulder.

"Let me get into position and I'll give you a shout; good luck." Moving off at a crouch to his right, Phil thought about how quiet he was, and that he was glad he would be up above them, watching their backs. Phil slowly moved down the line, catching the eyes of each man, who nodded in return, reaching Simon, who raised a thumb, and formed the OK sign with thumb and forefinger. Taking his place back at the front, the message came through: "Eyeball from Sierra One, permission." This was Steve.

"From Eyeball, go ahead."

"Sniper one on plot strike teams are clear to proceed."

Phil cupped one ear and listened.

"Total Team Alpha from Silver you have control."

Pausing for only a matter of seconds the reply was clear and direct. "From Total Alpha, yes, yes."

Edging forward, Phil could see the side gate to the waist-high wall to his front at about fifteen metres, and waved Simon's team through.

As the teams passed each other, Simon's last man turned to his right where Phil had crouched.

"Last man," he whispered. Simon had quietly slipped the gate open, and they entered lining up on the other side.

"Gate clear," he told Phil, who could move forward now; he could still feel the reassuring hand on his shoulder, and gentle squeeze.

Moving through the gate entrance, he could see Simon and his lads stood up, stacked against the whitewashed wall, to the left of the main door. The glass panels showed the interior hall lights, and clear view into the corridor. Slowly Phil led his team across the small grassy area and hugged the wall to his left; it felt warm and somehow comforting, as he moved his free left hand along it. Reaching the corner, he paused, and reassuringly still felt Reuben's hand on his shoulder. Peering around, he saw the light from two bay windows piercing through drawn curtains, lighting up the two vehicles that had been parked up. Keeping low, below the bay windows, the eight-man team approached the rear door, which was a wooden barn type door, split across the middle.

The teams now were crouching, and Reuben's hand left his shoulder as he passed to the right, and crossed the door, turning to face Phil. Tim's hand rested on his shoulder, and the sergeant was conscious of a Heckler and Koch MP5 level with his right eye pointing forward. It was quiet and reaching across to his left breast, he removed a stun grenade, and lowered his sub-machine gun, as he changed hands. In front of him, Reuben had tried the door handle, and finding it to be open, had opened the doors slightly, and placed a small wooden wedge under the bottom panel. Grenade in hand Phil keyed the radio.

"Stand by stand by... *go, go, go!*"

In a split-second Reuben had opened the door and thrown his first stun grenade which had been followed by Phil's. Behind him each of the other six had thrown the first of theirs, through the glass of the bay windows. The noise was deafening. Reuben turned and scanned the area in front as Phil rose and ran into the doorway, against the wall to the right; Tim moved with him on his left. The nine bangs were continuing, and Phil could hear the windows behind him shattering as each team member threw another, then another. The sound was deafening, and relentless. Phil scanned to his right, with the weapon. Despite the room being full of smoke from the explosions, the lights which had been left on pierced the room. Glancing to his left, Tim moved further into the room and dominated his half. Phil walked forward and could hear shouting and further nine bangs from the back of the house where Simon and his team were making their way further into the farmhouse. Beyond Phil was a door on the right, and Reuben pushed past and crouched, holding the handle and looking at Phil who was now opposite him, awaiting the squeeze from Tim. It was only a matter of seconds that the room had been cleared, and Tim squeezed his sergeant's shoulder. Again, the door was unlocked, and with one swift movement the door had been pushed aside and Reuben's second grenade was hurled forward. Phil's eyes were looking down the sight into the door as it was swung open, giving him a split-second clear view, as the second team set up beside him ready to enter. The first flash was blinding but he thought he could see figures diving to the floor and crouched holding their hands to their heads. It all appeared as if in slow motion, as another grenade flew past his left ear, and Mick and Rick entered, splitting at the doorway left and right. As the flashes and noise stopped, Phil and Tim entered the doorway, and saw that Mick and Rick had moved further on and were pointing their weapons to the figures on the ground, and shouting, "Armed police! Stay down! Keep still, keep still."

The radio crackled into life.

"Total Team Bravo we have six X-Rays in the living room!" It was Mick, screaming, in an adrenalin-fuelled tirade. Reuben pushed through extending his left hand with a bunch of plasti-cuffs and resting it on the left-hand man's right shoulder. It was Rick, and he stepped back slightly. Tommo and Steve entered, in quick succession and joined Reuben, slinging their weapons to their sides, grabbing the plasti-cuffs from Reuben's outstretched arm Tommo passed some to Steve, and started to handcuff the people on the floor. The shouting was relentless, but anyone could understand the clear instructions. Rick and Mick had spread left and right, scanning the prone figures with their weapons. Turning to his left Phil could see movement in the doorway. It was Simon. In what had only been a small number of minutes, his team had darted from room to room, clearing each one, until he had reached Phil and his teams.

Slinging his weapon to one side, he drew his Glock and walked into the room.

His radio was working overtime, and Phil interrupted with an update. Simon had not found any other people, so the seven were all accounted for. Vehicles were on their way to collect prisoners, and would be there soon, together other search teams, and detectives.

Looking down at the floor Phil counted the figures again. Reuben had been joined by members of Simon's team, and they were furiously searching and securing the prone prisoners.

Reuben turned to his sergeant and after getting his attention pointed to the person he had hold of.

His hands had been cuffed behind him, his face was turned away, and he appeared to be coughing. This person appeared to be much bigger than the others, and Phil squinted at Reuben as if to query what he wanted. Reuben rolled the person up and on to his feet. As he rose, his back was facing Phil, and the weapon that was extended to his front. Reuben tugged the arm he was holding, and the figure turned. The weapon remained steady aiming at the centre of the large chest as he faced him. Phil studied the face and spoke into his radio.

"All stations from Total Team Alpha, Tango one secured." Jo, who was helping the others, pulled another to his feet, and stood him beside Reuben. A smile spread across Phil's face.

"From Team Alpha, can confirm Tangos one and two secured."

Both Burns brothers had been caught, without a shot being fired. These so-called hard men had been caught cowering on a floor, shivering. Phil sniffed, and moved his balaclava to one side, sniffing again. Then it struck him one of them had messed himself. He had seen this before on other jobs, where pure fear had taken a hold. The radio told him vehicles were outside. Phil left the room and stood outside the doorway as Thomas Burns was led out by Reuben. A Range Rover was at the door with officers awaiting the cargo. As Burns left the doorway, his eyes fell on Phil whose pistol was levelled at him.

The police sergeant was not fazed at the unkempt dirty figure, and he moved closer. Pure evil, he often wondered whether it was something that a person was born with, or did it grow, fester, and develop inside a man until it could no longer be contained?

CHAPTER 21

The process of investigation and file building does not stop upon arrest, it is at that point when the challenging work and painstaking case building begins in earnest. This, of course, with a constant eye on the slow-ticking clock, straining to meet each time deadline, each salient point being examined in minute detail to ensure it's watertight. Senior officers attending closed doors meetings with barristers and judges, to ensure that the prosecution gets a safe and righteous conviction.

As well as the judicial decisions which were to be made, were the ones about the transportation and guarding of the brothers, throughout the entire process.

Intelligence poured in from all manner of sources. This ranged from members of the public, police officers, other police forces, and informants. Some of it was provided willingly, and occasionally for reward, by way of registered informants. It quickly transpired that the suspects and their associates were actively linked to the worst type of criminality, and its perpetrators spread across the country.

The crimes in which they were linked, and had been convicted, were almost all, without exception associated with violence.

One such report regarded a driver, who they used to drive them around the Southwest, when they had come down on an earlier crime spree. The driver, a middle-aged petty criminal, had met the brothers in a pub in an area of Plymouth called

Devonport, a couple of years previously, whilst three sheets to the wind on rough cider. Thomas Burns had overheard the man, bragging to some young lads playing pool about his fictitious criminal shenanigans, to try get another pint of sour apple juice. Burns had followed the man, Micky to the toilets, and waved twenty-pound notes in his face, saying there was more if he wanted it. Micky, of course, was interested and shook the big traveller's hand, agreeing to meet him and his brother Michael the following evening, in the pub's car park.

The next evening at nine o'clock, the pub was quiet and the scruffy excuse for a patron's car park was quiet, as Micky leant against the magnolia-stained wall, puffing on the smallest remnant of a rolled-up fag you could get, burning his bottom lip. The Burns brothers drove in past Micky and circling around pulled up alongside in a large wheel-based Mercedes Sprinter van.

Micky spat the fag out, and walked over to the driver's window, where Thomas was sat, staring ahead.

Michael stepped out, as the unsuspecting Micky approached the door, and walked around the front of the Mercedes, stopping at Mickey's right shoulder. Feeling the tall figure behind him, Micky swallowed hard, as Thomas explained what he wanted him to do. The brothers wanted a local driver with extensive knowledge of the area, in return for regular cash payments.

Micky agreed, and Thomas jumped out of the van, joining his brother. The pair dwarfed Mickey, who had started to wonder what he had got himself into. Michael placed his left hand on the shaking shoulder of the cider-sodden man to his front and leant forward to speak in his ear.

"We have not met, I know, and I speak on behalf of my brother as well. You ever fuck us over, ever, for anything, and we will do you, understand?"

A nervous Micky nodded, and the brothers laughed, as the shaking driver was shoved towards the waiting vehicle. Sitting in the van, he looked around the sparse cab, and back to the brothers.

"We'll be in touch, now fuck off, and go home. Lay off the drink and park the van out of sight near your flat."

They turned and entered the pub's rear fire escape. Micky gunned the accelerator and left the car park to drive home, showering the wall with wet soil and shingle.

Over the next six weeks, the new driver drove the pair and often nameless accomplishes, to locations throughout Devon and Cornwall. Often waiting in dark unlit muddy lanes for hours on end, never asking or querying, always ending with a grubby handful of notes shoved into his, as he dropped them off at the end of each job.

One Sunday evening, he had been asked to pick the pair up, who were with two others, from a Premier Inn, beside the A38, just on the outskirts of Plymouth. Arriving at 0300hrs, as instructed, he got out to open the doors. As he did, he was hit on his head, knocking him out at once.

He came to a short time later, to find himself tied and gagged, in the rear of the van, which was being driven. Two figures in dark clothing were sat beside him, smoking.

He lost consciousness again, but was jolted awake, as the van slid to a stop. Micky had no idea how long he had been out of it, but his head ached, and he felt a wet warmness at the base of his neck, as he tried to open his eyes. As much as he wanted to he could not open them, but he knew that there was nothing tied around his face. Rough hands picked him up under his armpits, and slammed him against the rear doors, which opened, and he fell out on to the cold soil on his side. The fall winded him, and he gasped for a breath. He heard voices, speaking in whispers a short distance away, and heard the engine of the van stop, and a door being slammed. His head was dizzy, and he felt scared.

Whilst unconscious, the two brothers had poured Super Glue, onto both of Mickey's closed eyes, much to the amusement of the two unnamed males, in the car park of the Premier Inn.

Mickey heard a flurry of movement, and slamming of doors, as the van pulled away and sped off into the distance.

The hapless driver never found out the reason the brothers did what they did, nor did he ever find out who the other two persons were. In any case he recalled that he was on the ground certainly until first light, when a Dartmoor ranger had stumbled across him. An ambulance took him to hospital for treatment where he remained for two weeks, being treated for an open fracture of his skull, and the effects of having his eyes superglued shut.

Upon his release from the Plymouth Hospital, he went straight to Charles Cross Police Station, and gave a statement detailing in every detail what he knew about the brothers and their activities.

Later, during the court case, his evidence was to become crucial and pivotal to their conviction.

CHAPTER TWENTY-TWO

During the months of court appearances, the suspects were to be produced from Bristol Prison, and driven down to The Crown Court at Exeter Castle. Because of their links to the criminal underworld there had been a very necessary requirement to treat them as Category A Prisoners. This linked with the use of firearms in the commission of the crime, meant that the prison van was escorted at high speed, by armed police and motorcyclists.

At the start of the court case, it was decided that the threats, perceived or otherwise, dictated that the two suspects were guarded, by Firearms Officers, before attendance, on route to, during and after. This was to occur for every court day.

The logistics were immense. Initially while the case was being prepared by both legal sides, Elite Firearms Officers spent days travelling several routes to and from the brothers' prison in Bristol to the court at Exeter.

It was decided that during the trial, each route would be chosen minutes before leaving the Bristol area, to lessen the opportunity of an attempted hold-up and escape.

Following much debate and confirmation of funding from government, the convoy and its cost implication was ratified and confirmed.

The convoy, known as a Category A convoy, used for only the most dangerous criminals, was a man- and vehicle-intensive operation, which had to run without any hitches.

It was decided that apart from the two suspects, and four prison guards, in their armoured prison van, sixteen Specialist Firearms Officers, and five police motorcyclists would be used. It later transpired that the motorcyclists would earn a fortune in overtime, throughout the trial.

On a damp Sunday morning in the indoor range at Police Headquarters, one week before the trial's commencement, forty authorised Firearms Officers were told to gather in the cramped classroom B.

The last officer had got his coffee and seated himself, as the door sprung open, and four familiar faces entered, with the compulsory blue A4-sized notebooks under their arms.

They took their positions at the chairs at the front of the room, and whilst three sat down, the fourth strode over to the windows and dropped the blinds.

There was a muted silence of anticipation, amongst the eager volunteers, as the last visitor took his place behind the desk.

The name plates in front of them remined every one of the wealth of experience, and knowledge that they had.

Sgt "Buzz" Offord was a veteran of the Firearms Teams, and a founder member was highly respected and revered. Inspector Derek Sandford was the new face of Firearms Command, and a transferee from the Metropolitan Police, a quiet but knowledgeable boss. Chief Inspector "Brum" Oldman, a no-nonsense 'go get them' Brummie transferee, with a ton of experience as a Firearms Officer, and still authorised, responsible for ordering all the kit and equipment, and looking after the boys. Finally, the big boss, and member of the management team, Superintendent Pounter, a serious and articulate professional, who was destined for the top.

Mr Pounter rose and cleared his throat.

"Ladies and gentlemen, welcome to the brief for Operation Curry Trail. What is said in this room today is confidential and shall remain so, throughout its duration. Before I start, can I just confirm that all the Firearms Officers present, are all currently authorised, and in possession of their Firearms Authorisation cards; if not, please say now. There was a slight murmur as faces looked around, and tried to note any movement, there was none.

"Right then, over to you Inspector Sandford."

The following two hours was broken by a coffee break and allowed for a quick visit to the toilets for those who needed it. The brief comprehensively laid out the plans and logistics for the production and transportation of the two suspects, from Bristol to Exeter, and back again.

The planning had been exhaustive, and the briefing was broken by numerous opportunities for questions, which were encouraged. Both Pete and Simon's teams were included and had been told they were there for the entirety of the tasking, as a 'thank you' for what they had done during the investigation already.

Towards the end of the presentation, a file in a beige waterproof folder titled 'Operation Curry Trail' in highlighted writing on the front was handed to every member of the audience, which outlined what had been said and more importantly how it was to be executed.

The police vehicles were to be the new white unmarked Range Rovers; each would hold four armed officers. Distributed amongst them was every conceivable piece of equipment, which could possibly be required, including enough assorted ammunition and flash bangs to start a small war.

Vehicle one would have the second in command, who would be the main map reader in the front passenger seat. Vehicle two had the same number of persons, one of whom was the convoy commander, who also had a map to follow, then the prison van, and remaining two Firearms vehicles with the firepower that goes with it.

The dress was civilian clothes, and blue baseball caps which were not to be worn until outside of the vehicles. The bulletproof vests had 'Police' written on the front and rear, with convenient flaps which hid them until needed. All weapons were to be loaded and made ready; safety catches applied.

There were to be half a dozen runs to and from the venues at high speed before the trial began. Management would throw in last-minute problems to evaluate the teams to their limits, catering for every eventuality.

Anything which either could, or did, slow it down became a hazard, and was to be communicated to every vehicle. Every order which was to be given would always be repeated, with every vehicle keeping close, and tight to the one in front and behind.

Throughout their presence at the court, Firearms Officers including Phil and Simon's teams would be deployed with covert weapons in plain clothes. Unusually two members would be sat in the back of the court, during the hearings, with concealed weapons, such was the perceived threat of an escape attempt.

CHAPTER TWENTY-THREE

The first day of the trial was upon them all, in no time. Hours and hours of relentless practice and rehearsal had brought them all up to an amazing level. There were numerous tasks, for everyone which changed on a day-by-day basis, with each team member knowing what to do inside out, and back to front.

The duty sheets had been circulated amongst every team member, in three-week stages.

Within the Firearms teams it was quite simply two teams every Monday to Friday, with different timings depending on which team you were on.

The team members concerned in the transporting of the suspects to and from were Bravo Team and had to be on the road to Bristol at 0600hrs each morning and returning at whatever time the trial finished each day.

Echo Team were the Firearms lads at Exeter Court, in Rougemont Castle, generally starting at 0800hrs on plot, again until the end of proceedings each day. These two teams swapped each week, and it was going to be exhausting and laborious.

Being the first day, both teams formed up in the range at Headquarters in Exeter. It was a dark and cold 0500hrs on the first of many Monday mornings. Reuben and the rest of the Exeter team were to be the transport and convoy teams, with Phil being the convoy commander, and Jason being the map reader. The prison van was already at the prison and would remain there when starting and finishing each day. The driver and two guards were from the prison and had been carefully selected. The van was one of the new G4s vans, used specifically for roles such as this, and had been checked over by Phil and Jason a week before.

As with most vans of this description, all the rear windows had been blacked out, and there was only enough room to accommodate two prisoners, plus prison staff. The designated staff for the van, again, had been specifically selected and vetted, to ensure that they were not likely to be susceptible to any coercion or bribery, leading to an escape attempt.

To some on the outside, all these precautions may have seemed excessive, but the intelligence that was being collected and filtered by the intelligence cell suggested that there was a very real threat to spring the two brothers, especially when it became known that there had been a substantial reward offered to any member of the underworld willing to attempt it, such was their influence and reputation.

As the shutters rolled up into the roof, the vehicles emerged into the chilly morning and parked up alongside the range building. The vapour from the four gleaming white Range Rovers drifted up and hung a little before drifting away. As they drew up behind each other, lights and blue strobes were activated, and a cackle of radio transmissions between each of the four vehicles confirmed that they were all working, they were in the correct sequence, and everyone knew their roles, and responsibilities inside out.

Although it was early, the guys who would be at the court emerged from the darkness of the range, and stood on the grassy knoll, beside the grey walls of the police canine school, and looked on admiringly, knowing that in a week's time the roles would be reversed, and that it would be them in the cars. It was important that everything went to plan.

Jason opened the door of the lead car, map in hand and strolled down to the second vehicle, where the front passenger door also opened, and Phil stepped out.

The mood was upbeat, and relaxed, with the teams shouting friendly obscenities to each other.

Windows were wound down, followed by an arm being thrust out displaying a single finger raised to the sky; typical, it was Rick. A loud chorus of laughter went up as the arm disappeared, and the window was wound up.

The officers on the knoll turned to their left, at the sounds of the motorcycle escort got louder, turning into the road ahead, weaving towards them all.

The five bikes were in full "Battenberg" livery, and all the riders were dressed in their brand-new high-vis reflective clothing and helmets. The bikes were the new BMW 1200cc bikes, tried and tested and very capable of the task ahead of them. One by one the bikes got to the end of the road and turned slowly until they were alongside the convoy. Each rider stopped their bike and remained seated with the engines idling. The front bike was being ridden by Chris, another ex-Royal Marine, and traffic officer who had been in the Department since the late eighties.

He raised his dark visor and leant to his left peering into the open window of the lead vehicle, where Jason was to be seated. Reuben was sat patiently, holding the steering wheel with both hands. Beside him to his left was his Heckler and Koch MP5, wedged into the gap between the seat's arm, and centre console. Reuben had loaded it with a thirty-round magazine and cocked it; his pistol was in his chest holster. On his right thigh was the sleeve, with assorted shotgun ammunition, just in case.

Chris leant closer.

"Morning Royal, expecting trouble?"

Reuben laughed and turned towards the biker. "Only you Chris, only you!"

As he spoke, Reuben recalled he had not been called Royal for some time. It was a friendly greeting between ex-Royal Marines, was used occasionally and with good humour. Chris looked over his right shoulder as he heard Jason walking up to the door and steadied himself on his bike.

"Morning Jason," he said as the map reader opened the door and got into the vehicle. Closing the door with a thud, he looked at Chris and grinned.

"Over to you mate, no pressure; doughnuts if you fuck up." Chris spoke into his mike, and gunned the powerful bike, accelerating away, and turning left at the junction, followed by another. Phil's voice broke the silence on the radio set in the car.

"Bravo Team, go, go, go." The rest of the bikes roared past the convoy as the four cars pulled away. The blue lights and flashing headlights all came on simultaneously, and the teams switched on for what was about to be an hour and half of heightened awareness and alertness.

As the cars exited the Headquarters' gates, the second motorbike had straddled the junction stopping traffic in both directions, and the rider, Tim, waved the speeding convoy through. Ahead of them, Chris was making ground, with his lights and sirens warning cars ahead of the approaching convoy. Reuben and the other drivers concentrated on keeping up with each other, but at the same time listening to commentaries on the headsets, and vehicle radios. It was funny that at times like this, when all this information and directions are flying about, each person's mind subconsciously identifies which information or transmission is pertinent to the job in hand or the individual.

Accelerating hard, and turning left, the cars joined the

A3015, and headed towards Junction 30 of the M5. Reuben glanced to his right to see a blur as the third bike passed him to take up position at the impending roundabout, to enable the waiting bike to continue ahead. This is how they worked, and they worked hard, leapfrogging each other to ensure a smooth and uninterrupted high-speed journey.

Within the rear of each of the vehicles the otherwise redundant armed officers were scanning everything around them, looking for what could be a hazard or potential threat, most importantly suspicious vehicles or persons. When something was identified as an actual or potential hazard, it was communicated on the airwaves, so the drivers were always recalculating positions in the road speeds and alternative actions. An intense course of defensive driving and a week with Range Rover UK, had given them an exhaustive knowledge of the cars' capabilities, which were, by everyone's admission, astonishing. They had been taken over rough terrain and topped out on the long winding circuits of the test track.

As the convoy approached Apple Lane junction, which was on the right, traffic had been halted, and the radio crackled: "Caution, caution; pedestrians on the centre island, centre male pointing to us on his phone."

Reuben saw the group to his front and noted that the male mentioned had a young lad holding onto his left hand, with a female stood beside him as well. As the male was pointing Reuben turned on the wailing sirens, and the young boy waved. Safely through, they entered the roundabout at junction 30, in the lane for the M5 North, and Bristol. The bikes weaved in amongst them and the traffic like angry wasps, engines screaming through the gears.

As they climbed the slip road, the speed increased, and two

bikes edged out into the joining lanes to implement a rolling stop. Reuben looked down at the speedo which showed a leisurely eighty-five miles per hour. In his mind he knew that when the prison van was included, the speed would more likely be seventy, although it had been de-restricted for the job in hand.

Once all the convoy was on the motorway, Reuben eased the lead vehicle over to the third lane, and all the cars closed, settling in to the journey ahead.

The journey seemed to go very quickly with most other road users paying attention to what was storming up behind them. The weather had warmed, and the road conditions were perfect; it was a great start to what was going to be a frantic and drawn-out experience for all.

The banter within and among all the cars escalated, via the personal radios, which had been given their own dedicated channel. As the trial continued, this would be altered to ensure security and privacy. As always, the conversations turned to the team's stomachs, and brown paper bags were handed out to everyone containing a plentiful assortment of chocolate, biscuits, crisps, and the ever-important Cornish Pasty.

Phil in the second car had been on the phone for most of the journey, updating and in turn getting updated. All the bosses wanted this first day to run smoothly, no hitches, and it had done exactly that, almost too good to be true. Phil rang Jason's phone, which was hooked up to the hands-free set-up. It rang, and Reuben pressed the accept button on the steering wheel.

"Jason, Reuben, we leave at junction 18, signposted Avonmouth B4054, and this is when well earn our money. Everyone has got to be on the ball, and if necessary, drop off the speed; we cannot afford to split the vehicles up. We will be entering the built-up areas shortly after."

Jason acknowledged the message and Phil rang the other two vehicles giving them the same message. Food was stowed, the crews sat up, and switched on, and eager eyes scanned their arcs outside.

The convoy passed the 300-yard chevrons to junction 18, and Reuben indicated to turn off. Glancing in his rear-view mirror, he could see that the others had also done this. Slowing down gradually, he led the team on to the slipway, which climbed up towards a sharp left bend, joining the road, signposted Avonmouth and Bristol City Centre. The commuting traffic had got heavier; with it came the white van man, and Sunday morning drivers, although it was Monday.

Reuben was forced to drive more aggressively, with much flashing of headlights and tailgating. He could see the arms in vehicles ahead retract from the lazy driving positions, and some instinctively dropping their mobile phones, upon noticing a police vehicle was right behind them.

"I'm almost tempted to note down the registration numbers and report them later Reuben."

"As long as they're not talking about us," replied the occupied driver, and he laughed.

The bikes began to work overtime and were good at it. Their presence on the road was imposing, and gave motorists plenty of time, and left them in no doubt as to what was needed.

Jason and Phil had prepared several routes just in case, with all of them written down with directions, on their laps. Known as routes A, B, C, D, E, they were currently on route A.

Their convoy was expected, and small groups of people had gathered at pinch points, with mobile phones held up to record the cars and their arrival. The information being passed through the cars' radios had reached its height as the turned into

Cambridge Road 200 metres from the front of the prison. Avon and Somerset CCTV had followed the team as soon as they joined the road into Avonmouth, and they also had an officer sat beside the Controller with a hand-held radio, a direct link to Phil and the cars. Their CCTV covered the route all the way in, and they could direct or advise them accordingly. Luckily today it was unusually clutter and accident free. At the junction of Cambridge Road, a message had already been sent and received, and the gates at the entrance to the Prison Compound which ran into the basement level began to open. Armed officers, and members of Avon and Somerset Police Force sprang into action and enforced those already in position. One by one, the four vehicles turned into the approach and entered the underground reception area. As soon as the last one passed through, the gates were already closing, accompanied by the armed officers.

The vehicles turned in the basement staying in the same order, flanking the already stationary prison van, and facing towards the large, closed gates. As each car reached its position, the engines were turned off and doors began to open. One by one all the team alighted from their respective vehicles, stretching, and brushing their vests to clear away the flakes of pasty debris, and breadcrumbs and crisps.

Phil let out a loud whistle led by an arm gesture indicating all to gather round. As the last man closed in, Phil spoke.

"Well I hope every trip goes as well as that. Any points observations or questions?"

There was a pause and Rick from the rear vehicle 'tail-end Charlie' cleared his throat.

"Yeah, no problems really, if I can just say that when a message is passed, I should really be the last to confirm, rather than it be a bun fight, just saying."

Mick discreetly dug him in the ribs, so no one could see.

"Please, Miss," he whispered, and those who heard giggled.

"Yes," said Phil. "Make that a defo," and thanked him. "If there is nothing else, stow your weapons in the vehicles; it's secure in this area. Have a piss, dump and hot wet (drink) and be back here ready to go in twenty minutes."

CHAPTER TWENTY-FOUR

Thomas and Michael Burns had been deliberately kept apart for the months they had been on remand. They had been given different mealtimes, and on occasions eaten on their own.

They had received regular visits from a stream of barristers and solicitors, where they pleaded their innocence and tried to intimidate and bully anyone who would listen.

The intel section in the prison had consulted closely with the intel unit at Police Headquarters in Exeter with any information that was forthcoming about the twins. Even in prison people were all too eager to tell tales for certain privileges, such as cigarettes, mobile phone usage, or increased visits. Some of these conduits had let slip that the twins had quickly developed an aura of brutish thuggery within their wings and had taken to training regularly in the prison gym, bulking up quite dramatically in the process. Thomas had, over time leant on the 'hard men' and enforced his rule, and people feared them, aided by their reputation which preceded their incarceration.

Thomas was able to get a message to his brother written on a piece of cloth and concealed in the bottom of a drug-dependent long termer. Thomas had made it clear that they should keep their hard image, talking to only their briefs and counsels, whilst maintaining their innocence.

Monday saw them rise as normal, and enter the normal routine of washing, sluicing out, and breakfast. Unusually they ate at the same time, with Thomas sat about five metres away facing Michael, who was on a plastic chair, and who initially did not notice the more dominant brother staring. Michael took a mouthful of tasteless cereal and glanced up. Thomas!

For what seemed like minutes, the brothers stared at each other, and Michael raised his eyebrows, giving a slow, deliberate nod. Thomas raised his hand to his mouth and wiping it raised his thumb before dropping his head and continuing with the undercooked bacon and an excuse for scrambled egg. Less than ten minutes later both were in their cells, blocks apart, preparing the start of their journey, and the start of the trial.

Thomas had arranged casual clothes, to be delivered which were unlike the usual grubby unwashed and oil-stained jeans he would habitually wear. His brother had done the same.

As he dressed, Thomas looked in the stained metal mirror taped to the wall of his cell. The early morning shave and haircut which he had paid for the day before, was a complete transformation. Unfortunately, he could not do nothing about the stained and buckled teeth, a legacy of a rough childhood and playground scuffles. Michael did not fare any better, nor did he care. As he pulled on his jumper, Thomas straightened the collar of the polo shirt underneath and did not notice the odour that emanated from under his arms.

His shoes were plain, with no laces, comfortable and cheap with no style; a vast difference to the rigger boots he wore all the time.

As the brothers readied themselves, Phil had finished chatting to the prison staff and Avon and Somerset bobbies. Shaking their hands, he gulped the coffee down and excused himself to go to the toilet. As he entered, Jason had just stood at the dryer to dry his hands, and Phil tapped the back of his legs with his foot, causing the poor old preoccupied chap to buckle, almost dropping to the floor.

"Twat," said Jason as he turned to see the grinning skipper and laughed.

Phil continued to the urinal and listened as Jason started the dryer.

"This should be interesting, Phil; we haven't seen these two dickheads since we nicked them," Jason shouted above the drone of the dryer. Phil zipped up his jeans and turned, walking to the wash basin beside Jason and the wall-mounted machine, hesitating and holing each side of the basin, as he turned to Jason.

"I know that we have done a decent job, but there is still a lot more to do. A lot of people will be looking at us, but this is going to be an interesting couple of weeks or even months."

Turning on the tap, Phil bent over and liberally splashed his face, gasping at the chilly water. Outside the convoy group were positioned in order of travel. The prison van was positioned within the convoy, engine running, with the open side door and steps closest to the prison entrance. Phil appeared from another door talking with Jason and stopped beside the prison van, as Jason assumed his position in is car.

Phil and a guard spoke briefly, and he gestured to Martin to join him. Stepping out of the car, he bent over to Phil.

"Reuben, just cover this point with me as the customers get in the van."

Reuben dressed back and cradled his MP5. Phil joined him as the door was opened, and another guard appeared, trailing his extended right hand behind him, as he strode into the courtyard. Within seconds the first handcuffed brother appeared, his left wrist attached to the guard in front. His right arm hung loosely to his side, staying there as he took the few long steps, into the fresh air. Reuben looked at the figure that appeared, it was the tall figure of Michael. He took in as much visual information as he could, and fingering the Pressel switch on his radio, informed the team that subject two, Michael, was out, out, passing a brief description of his clothing. As quickly as he was out, he had climbed the steps and disappeared out of view inside.

Phil followed the pair into the van, straddling the door, as the brother was placed in his cell, and the door was closed. Turning to exit the door he jumped down the steps and turning to Reuben, gave thumbs up. Reuben relayed the information again and turned his attention to the prison entrance, giving Phil a returned thumbs up, as the last unit, Rick, in tail-end Charlie responded to the broadcast. Reuben felt his heart race, and grip on his weapon tighten, as the second guard appeared, again with his right arm extended to his rear. Thomas Burns appeared but at a much slower pace than his brother. He was as big as Reuben remembered, but had bulked out, due to the exceptional gym equipment provided by the taxpayer. As he cleared the door, his head turned to the right, and at only a distance of three or four metres, stared into Reuben's eyes. It seemed like minutes, and Reuben focused hard on the sly grin that appeared on the pockmarked face, revealing the stained and rotten teeth within. As quickly as he had turned his head, he again disappeared into the van, and Reuben heard him shout some inaudible comment to his brother, which was greeted by Michael banging the inside of the van repeatedly for about five seconds. Phil appeared, and the first stage was completed. A message from the prison crew confirmed they were ready, and Phil and Reuben assumed their positions in the Range Rover.

A quick radio check confirmed everyone was ready, and the convoy started to move as the prison's heavy shutter started to roll up, letting the warm air and sunlight stream in.

The route back to Exeter Court would not be the same, and the lead vehicle ensured that the communications confirming the directions were continuous and acknowledged. The communications centres at the Bristol CCTV, Avon and Somerset Police Headquarters, and Exeter, all knew at the last minute the route selected, and all available cameras were keyed up to keep watch when the convoy appeared. All eyes scanned the many groups of people at pinch points, and prominent road junctions, looking for the very real threat of an assault, or ambush.

It had been agreed that the prison staff in the van would give regular welfare checks, whilst travelling, and this continued throughout the journey.

The sight of this high-speed multiple vehicle convoy was impressive and professional, with the bikers again earning their wages, and some. They pushed the bikes to their absolute limits, weaving between vehicles with inches to spare, without giving it a second thought, occasionally raising their helmet visors to shout commands at motorists who were too slow, or unobservant.

The roads were unusually quiet, and joining the motorway, was quicker than expected, bringing a satisfying smile to not only the map reader but also Phil. A good start to the coming weeks, or months ahead. As Reuben gunned the Range Rover, he found himself glancing at Phil, sat beside him, who was busy speaking into and using two mobile phones, the radio and vehicle radio set, whilst reading the map, which was open on his lap. He admired Phil, whom he got on well with, and often had a beer with when off duty. He was aware that Phil had turned down a position of inspector at Headquarters to stay on the team, and in fact had decided to see his few remaining years off in his current role.

Turning his attention back to the task in hand, Reuben looked in his wing mirror, and saw the bikers beside the prison van, which was doing well to keep up. The regular checks with the prison guards inside, confirmed the van was holding its own, and the two brothers inside had settled into the journey without a word.

CHAPTER TWENTY-FIVE

Thomas Burns looked out of the darkened windows, at the cars that the van passed, oblivious to the violent and threatening cargo, which was on route to Exeter.

The dominant brother felt at ease and stretched out smoothing the jacket he had taken off and laid across his lap. His legal team which had changed as many times as he cared to remember, had been paid well, and had tried to get them bailed on numerous occasions without success. The last meeting had not gone well and had sent the brothers into a ferocious argument questioning what the team were doing. The evidence was largely circumstantial. hinging on the evidence of the main witness, who had been persuaded to turn Queen's evidence, with a promise of a reduced sentence. The brothers felt that the legal team should concentrate more on the integrity of the witness, a low-level persistent offender from Plymouth.

Burns had already decided that he would sort him out, regardless of the outcome, either at his hands or some other who would accept the payment he would offer, when the time came. He sniggered at the thought; he knew Albanians that would kill him for the cost of a long weekend in Prague or Warsaw and do a decent job of it as well. He closed his eyes and quickly drifted off, into a murky world of sex and violence, in another place, at another time.

The convoy ate the motorway miles up, until it only seemed an hour before they were a mile away from Junction 29

Southbound on the M5, the first turning taking them into Exeter City Centre

Rick, the map reader in the lead vehicle, gave everyone the heads-up, receiving acknowledgement from each car, including the prison van. Three of the bikes screamed forward at full tilt, to guard the junctions and stop the traffic. In unison the sirens started up as they descended the slip road, crossing the junction, and turning right against the red lights. Young children were seen to wave, and mouth observations to their parents, as the convoy breezed past under the traffic gantry signposted 'Exeter City Centre'. Windows opened at the newly built Met Office building across the road, as people rose from their seats to see what was happening.

At the court Team Bravo were ready and in position. All were in casual clothes, apart from the two selected to sit in the court who were dressed in blazers and chinos.

The route into Exeter was a slight descent, and the noise of the sirens carried a long way. Ears pricked up as the Bravo Team started to hear the convoy weaving its way towards them.

Coffee and teacups were quickly discarded, and jackets and blazers were adjusted, to ensure all weapons remained covert. It just happened to be that the teams made up of mainly ex-military, and the bosses had realised this at the planning stage, prompting an internal email, banning military ties and tie pins. The main reason for this was that if the media were able to obtain a photo of one of the team, it would be easier to try to identify and name him or her.

The convoy turned left into Castle Street, with barely a bumper's gap between them. The two lead bikes roared into the courtyard through the large Norman arch and shot left to give a clear passage. The first two Range Rovers followed, accelerating up to the side entrance and splitting at the last moment, forming a funnel for the prison van, which drove through, and onwards to the reception party at the open gates. As the last vehicle and motorbikes entered, Bravo reception Team took over, after Phil had broadcast the convoy's arrival over the net.

The van had pulled up alongside the side entrance, which was in an inner compound, but visible through fencing, twelve feet high. Two members of Bravo closed the inner cordon gates and turned and faced the courtyard.

After a short time, a matter of seconds, the doors of the van and the court side entrance opened in unison. The first guard appeared at the foot of the step plate with the first brother Michael in tow, and as soon as he appeared, he disappeared into the building, followed by the slower Thomas, who tried to look around him, but was forced to look down as he nearly tripped. The door slammed behind him, and two gate guards gave a thumbs up.

"Alpha and Bravo Teams stand down, stand down. The subjects are delivered and secured," said Phil calmly into his radio, prompting a sequential confirmation acknowledging the message.

"All units gather at the vehicle park for a debrief," came Phil's response. Within less than seven or eight minutes, all the personnel had gathered in a semi-circle to the rear of the convoy vehicles.

The high Roman walls of the historic Court building kept curious eyes at bay, and there was good cover from view.

Phil lowered the tail gate of the Range Rover and climbed up.

"Close in people, I don't really want to shout."

The group closed in, and mixed well, with some who had

already got a hot wet, or bottle of water in hand.

"Well, we are here!" exclaimed Phil. "Good job, fucking excellent job, all of you. Unless I am mistaken, all went well; do you have points for me?" He looked around as he could see each member going over the last two hours or so in their heads. The adrenalin was still flowing, and Phil sensed it, just by the quietness, and looks in the eyes of his gathered audience.

Turning his head to his left, his gaze settled on the group of motorcyclists, and could see that it had been a hard job for them

"How was the convoy from a bike perspective?" the question was not aimed at any particular person, but Chris, answered, unprompted.

"Yep generally it was good; the drivers need to be checking the wing mirrors all the time though, it got a bit tight at times. Motorway and A roads were fine, just the built-up areas. No need to hang around for us we will always make up the gaps."

Phil turned his attention to the main group whilst nodding in agreement.

"Good point, and I agree; anything else?" The group remained silent.

"OK lads. Bravo Team, over to you. Alpha Team get your kit sorted, vehicles fuelled, and chill."

Within the courtyard just past the entrance, was the café/canteen, which had been taken over by the teams for the duration of the trial, much to the absolute delight of the sisters who had owned it for over fifteen years. The money which had been negotiated as a retainer and paid upfront had multiplied their normal takings seven-fold, on top of the products and tea and coffee that would be bought by the officers.

CHAPTER TWENTY-SIX

The retaining cells in the depths of the old court building had been painted recently, and the sweet smell hung in the air. Provision had been made to accommodate the prison escort, with tables and a drinks machine, situated in the corridor.

The Burns Brothers had not been given the slightest chance of speaking with each other and had been placed in their cells quickly and without a hitch.

The legal counsels were already waiting for them, bundles of paperwork under their arms, chatting amongst themselves, and exchanging notes.

Thomas sat on the elevated bench and surveyed the four walls. He wanted to get on with it, and the smell of the fresh paint was getting to him, making his throat dry. Looking up and opposite the door, he saw a slim line of windows approximately a foot wide and three feet across: thick glass windows containing wire, and frosted, about nine feet up from the bench, and fronted by short thick bars. He guessed that they would be level with the floor of the courtyard above.

Michael was prone on his bench, arms folded under the back of his neck, legs crossed, thinking of all the people that had been in this very same room before, and what had happened to them, before drifting off into a sound sleep.

Thomas got up and strode over to the steel door and knocked loudly. Seconds later the viewing flap was dropped, and he leant over to look at the face of the guard staring back at him.

"Any chance of a cuppa, and biscuit?"

The guard smiled.

"Sugar? Sorry there aren't any biscuits, but lunch will be in a couple of hours."

Burns sighed, nodded and backed up, sitting down again. The flap remained open, and Thomas could hear talking outside, but could not make out what was being said.

Michael's eyes opened to the sound of knocking at his door. He looked over at the inspection hatch; it opened, and the same guard asked him if he too wanted a hot drink.

"No," came the impolite, abrupt response, and he closed his eyes again.

Several miles away, and oblivious, to the court activities Phil had drunk his second lukewarm cup of coffee quickly and walked over to Reuben who was sat with the boys, looking at a road map, which Jason had spread on the joined tables.

The sergeant nodded in Reuben's direction, who returned the nod, made his apologies then rose and joined the skipper as he left the room again. Emerging into the fresh air, they walked over to the parked vehicles, where they stopped and leant on the bonnet of the first Range Rover.

"Reuben, can you find the guys, get them rounded up, and take them and the cars back to Middlemoor? Give them a wash and clean and stay there until I ring."

Phil explained that he would stay at the court on this the first day and help Bravo Team with the court duties, Reuben nodded and the pair split to go their separate ways.

Bravo Team's role whilst the court sat was quite simple, and as the trial went on, it became laborious.

The weather forecast had been obtained from the Met office weeks before the commencement of the trial, and so far, had been correct. It was baking hot, and the wearing of blazers and suit jackets for Bravo Team would go on to be a real issue.

When the brothers had been delivered safely to the court, there was a small window of time when Bravo Team's transition was set in motion.

People who have never been involved in anything like this would think it is like what happens in the films. Macho, tough, exciting, and non-stop action, when it could not be further from the truth.

People trained in this skillset expect to be bored and static, for extended periods of time, waiting for the one time they may have to put it all to effective use. Invariably it will never ever be used, and deep down, they want it that way. The secret is to never switch off.

Within the Firearms teams, there was the ability, knowledge, and equipment to deal with most things firearms related. The guarding or escorting of persons or suspects whilst armed on a smaller scale, would be undertaken by the Close Protection teams, especially with high-profile people like those in government, the Royal family, etc.

On an operation such as this, within the teams were guys who were trained Close Protection officers, and their input was always welcome, and listened to. Equally many of them had undertaken what was arguably the most demanding Close Protection course in the world, the one run for the military in Liphook, Hampshire. This is where military personnel from around the world went to, the majority being Military Police personnel. The certification you got at the end of it was a qualification for life, and carried significant clout for potential future employers.

The dress code for guarding at the court had been discussed

with both counsels and the judge in closed meetings. It had been thought that an informal, almost casual dress sense, whilst carrying firearms, would not sit well with the media and public.

Individuals had still to wear equipment that would make the hot days uncomfortable, and hotter.

Under each shirt each officer would be wearing his, or her personal issue, body armour, radio harness, and holster for their weapon. Generally, most opted for the easy and lightweight 'YAKI' slide, which holstered their self-loading pistols with ease on their waistbands. A couple of the more experienced ranking officers still used underarm shoulder holsters, which served the purpose equally well.

The PYE radio comms setup, with collar microphones and palm transmitters, had to be threaded through shirts and jackets. The main wire loops were taped onto the body armour, hidden from view, with fresh batteries, as were the skin-coloured wireless earpieces. Each of these was worth about £300 and stayed with each officer, due to the cost and health implications. Of course, this meant that the opportunity to take one's jacket off and chill was not an easy thing to do without displaying what lay underneath. To this end, the Force had commandeered the court's carpark attendant's cabin, which was ideally situated within the courtyard. Making the most of what was to hand was a skill all the team members had, and rotas were quickly set up to rotate from the cabin, which also doubled up as a meal room.

Reuben and his team arrived at the range after dropping off the two brothers, watched by Phil, and guarded by Bravo Team.

Throughout the trial, all training and use of the range had been suspended. This enabled the vehicles to park without any interruptions, and the teams could chill and de-rig, out of sight of keen and eager eyes.

CHAPTER TWENTY-SEVEN

The case was predicted to last for eight weeks, unofficially, but each of the team members knew that it would be more like twelve. It transpired that the verdict was delivered in the middle of the thirteenth week, after a jury deliberation of only one day.

Throughout the trial, the press had remained in large groups, which grew as the weeks passed, aided by the continual rantings and animated performances from both brothers. These often resulted in one or both being ejected on the direction of the judge for contempt of court. At one point this became so bad that the brothers were not allowed to attend, unless necessary, for a whole week, whilst counsels were arguing points of law.

The Firearms Officers who rotated duties in the public gallery would attract an audience of colleagues at the end of each day, as they relayed the behaviour of the two overconfident brothers and their resulting court punishments.

Their defending barristers were regular visitors to the judge's chambers, to be told off, or given directions by the judge, in relation to their client's behaviour. This behaviour in front of an elected jury went some way to condemning them if there was any doubt at all.

Although mostly circumstantial, it was damning, and was cemented by the evidence given by the main prosecution witness, a Plymouth-based middle-aged man, known as witness A1, who gave evidence by way of a video link from a secure location, somewhere in the UK.

Witness A1 was a man called Chris Curnow, born in Devonport Plymouth in the early sixties; he was one of six children, bought up by a diligent single parent. The family was doomed from the start. Money was scarce, and education was not enforced due to Mum being absent from her children for all the daylight hours. It became the burden of the two oldest children, Chris and his older sister Abby, to look after their younger siblings, to feed and clothe them.

The seven of them survived on little, cramped into a one-bedroomed terraced house, which had received a hammering during the Blitz, over twenty years before. The repairs had been hurried, and not fit for purpose. The damp and infestation were almost beyond liveable, and it was apparent in the bouts of illnesses, and raucous coughing, which echoed throughout the day and night, that it would take its toll.

It was when Chris, aged ten years, found his mother's lifeless body beside him one cold frosty morning, in the shared bed, that his life spiralled into the darkest depths of despair and need.

The young family were split, and the siblings were never to see each other again.

The young Chris was sent to a strict orphanage on the outskirts of Plymouth, run by veterans of the last war, almost Borstal-like in its regime. He quickly fell into bad company, and learnt the finite skills of defending yourself, and burglary, which were to stay with him for life.

His life had been altered and would be the cause of numerous prison stays in his teenage years. He gained a reputation of being violent, and unpredictable, fuelled by an insatiable appetite for alcohol of every description. This need for it increased his criminality, making him steal from other like-minded individuals. This resulted in many disputes, and physical punishments, at the hands of paid thugs, who were good at their job. Chris was to carry the scars of many beatings with him forever.

This reputation and history bought him along the road that led to him being introduced to the two brothers, who would also change his life forever.

From the start, it was obvious why the two London criminals had decided to use the ageing Curnow, to be the driver and runaround. His knowledge of rich pickings and easy targets had been drawn from a lifetime of criminal associations, and storytelling whilst at Her Majesty's pleasure. The honing and expansion of skills and techniques continued throughout.

His criminal exploits had settled onto burglary and crept more into the rural parts of Devon and then Cornwall, with the rare excursion cross-border entries into Dorset and Somerset, to steal agricultural equipment, and horse-related items.

He had access to, and knew well, the big fish who would pay handsomely for his ill-gotten gains, for a handful of readies, no questions asked. As his addictions grew, his ability at negotiating fair prices diminished, and the handlers knew this, resulting in little money for expensive items, in the quest for the next bottle of vodka, or whiskey, and most recently the white devil, cocaine.

The brothers knew this and played with his addiction cajoling him into more and more audacious plots, in more obscure locations.

He had been sat on his own on a stool in the Dray Arms on Plymouth Quay one Tuesday evening. At the weekends, the Dray was a popular haunt for all the Armed Forces on a night out in Plymouth, because it had four giant TV screens to show all the sport, on any day.

On this evening, Curnow had not been needed by the brothers who had gone back to London for a week, to attend an extended wake of a good friend. Having been bunged a monkey to tide him over, he had drunk almost a third of it the day before, knocking cheap whiskey and double vodkas down until he could not remember the evening.

As he sipped on the straight house double, he glanced up at the screen in front of him. The pub was still and quiet, and he could hear the presenter talking about Wadebridge, and he squinted to take in the images, as he knew the area well.

The programme was about people who had moved into rural areas, having worked or lived in the hub and bustle of a city such as the nation's capital, London.

The camera switched to a signpost showing Wadebridge, and a gravelled drive. Curnow stood up glass in hand and walked towards the large screen to hear and see better.

The smiling faces of Tilly Light, and her mother Sally filled the screen, as they stood beside the open doors into the workshop behind them.

Curnow placed the glass on the table beside him, and reached into his right-hand trouser pocket, taking his phone out, holding it limply at his side.

The two ladies had moved their extraordinarily successful business down to Cornwall to continue with their bespoke furniture enterprise, and at the same time take in everything that this lovely part of the country had to offer.

The reports of their success – indeed the growth of their company – with images of products priced in their thousands prompted Curnow to dial in a number and raise the phone to his ear.

Without taking his eyes off the screen, he began to speak

"It's me, you need to get back here, I've found a peach of a job."

CHAPTER TWENTY-EIGHT

Initially there was truly little to go on, within the investigation. Whoever had done this had done it with a clear lust for violence.

Those that knew mother and daughter, knew that they would not have offered any resistance, and were slight in build.

The level of violence culminating in their deaths had been extreme.

As with all instances like this, informants were contacted and met to try to find who had been responsible.

Clandestine meetings and passing over of money occurred throughout Devon and Cornwall. There was a belief still, that there is a code of conduct, unwritten, almost an honour amongst criminals, which should prompt someone to step forward and supply that one piece of information to put detectives on the trail of those responsible.

There is a computer indexing system used by police forces, nationally known as HOLMES (Home Office Large Enquiry System). The officers who input and receive the information to input would have to have attended and passed a course, to be able to set up and run the system and are known as indexers. Quite simply, all information that was received by any means would be typed into the data base, and the computer would generate an 'action'. This was simply a tasking with a unique reference number. Enquiring officers would be given this action, and its reference number, to conduct the enquiry, update it, and resubmit it. This in turn, of course, may have led to further information being revealed, requiring further enquiries, so another action would have been generated.

Snippets of information started to dribble in from numerous sources, chatter here, chatter there, and someone heard someone say something.

People have different and varied reasons for passing information to the authorities. Sometimes it is because it pulls at certain strings such as moral reasons, or levels of violence used, or even the persons who are the victims. Certainly this job touched all those and more.

The common theme of these pieces of information was the mention of two brothers from the London area, who were feared, and who were using local criminals not only for their local knowledge, but also to transport them from one crime to another. More importantly, they were staying somewhere in Devon, in a remote farm complex.

Detectives who scanned all the information were frustrated, as they felt they were close, but just needed a name, or an address.

The murders had attracted substantial press coverage, not only locally, but nationally, in the local rags, radio, and local and national television.

Members of the victims' family were given time on TV to appeal for information leading to the arrest and conviction of whoever was responsible. Their speeches were moving and sad, accompanied by photos of the two victims in happier times,

The jury on whether this is a good thing to do is generally regarded as being out, by most as generally it seems that the very people who are broadcasting turn out to either be the offenders or those who know who the offenders are.

Colin Step had been a police officer for over twenty years, and had joined Exeter police, as it was then known, as a cadet, spending most of his career on traffic; he was a very experienced and knowledgeable man.

It was in the early nineties that he realised that an effective way of earning stacks of overtime was to undertake a HOLMES indexer's course. The officers who were already trained were used on every major incident, and would work if they wanted, racking up hundreds of hours in overtime and time off.

There was one particularly nasty, yet still ongoing murder of a young schoolgirl, where the indexers were earning so much overtime, that they were having major work done on houses and buying new cars.

Colin soon realised that the course was not as easy as he first thought, and initially he was not the quickest at typing in and indexing all the information.

Early deployments in the role showed the amount of intelligence that needed examination, calibration and inputting.

It was crucial to highlight any potential relevant and duplicated intelligence, which needed immediate attention. He soon found out that the hours and long days, impacted massively on his day-to-day life, and more importantly, his sleep patterns.

Three months later, the routines and duties in the indexers' rooms were second nature now. This situation was helped by an unusual rise in major enquiries, and a shortage on similarly trained staff.

Colin was single, and had no partner to answer to at home, so he decided to make hay while the sun shone, and rake the overtime, and time in lieu days while he could. He could already sense a new car on the horizon.

He had been brought onto the murder of mother and daughter, relatively late, about a month into it.

The rudiments and rooms had been well established, and

indexers had been smashing the keys, to favourable effect, filtering and prioritising all the information at an alarming rate.

This Monday, Colin had travelled down to Cornwall, with another indexer from Exeter, 'Dixie' Dean, an experienced officer with many years under his belt. He hailed from East Devon, where he was the Neighbourhood Officer for Budleigh Salterton, and had been for more than eight years.

Arriving at the HOLMES room situated handily next to the Major Incident Room, Colin took his seat opposite Dixie. Pulling his chair up, he placed his hot coffee with two sugars onto the blue notebook to his right, and yawned, loudly extending his arms out to his side.

Settling into his high-backed chair, he turned his computer on, leant back whilst the computer booted up. Looking around, he saw that Dixie was on the phone, and oblivious to all that was going on around him.

Colin looked to his left and studied the three-tier tray system, marked with the typical in, out, pending. There was just one tray to his right. Of them all this was the important one. This was where he would put any 'urgent' actions, or anything that he felt needed immediate attention.

A room 'runner' periodically went from desk to desk, collecting these and taking them to the Senior Officer on duty.

Colin had developed a system, where he would jot down notes on a small A5 pad, of anything he felt was strange, important or just worthy of note.

It was an easy and personal way of recalling things without interrogating the police computer.

The screen blinked into action before him, and entering his username and password, started the long day.

He had been at his desk for about two and a half hours, and

Colin had beavered feverishly on the dozens of actions which had landed in his tray.

Suddenly he stopped and his fingers hovered over the keyboard, moving his now cold and empty coffee cup to one side he stretched out and picked up his notebook.

He held the book clasped in both hands as he stared at the screen, carefully digesting the text.

"The name, the name," he kept repeating to himself under his breath.

"Dixie," he called over to the figure, opposite him, hunched over typing away.

Dixie looked up and replied, "Can I help you, buddy?"

"Have you had anything into today about that Devonport scrote, supposedly driving those London gypsies around?"

Dixie placed his elbows on the desk, and looked up to the ceiling, pausing.

"Not that I'm aware, he said, dropping his gaze to look at his mate. "Fancy a coffee?"

Colin nodded, as Dixie rose and came over to him. Raising his cup, he extended his arm.

"Cheers mate."

Dixie disappeared into the kitchen and Colin heard the switch of the kettle above the hustle of the enquiry room.

Staring at the screen he read the text again.

The local Plymouth bloke who is driving for the London brothers is called Chris Curnow, an alcoholic. He was the driver when they killed the two women in Cornwall.

Colin thumbed the pages of his notebook. *There it is!* he thought. Sliding his right index finger down the open pages, he stopped at an entry which had been highlighted and read it again.

Local criminal driving for major burglars from London is

called Chris from the docks is in Plymouth.

Looking back at the screen he printed it off and noted the action number in his notebook and printed it off as well.

Rising from the chair he walked to the printer which was to the left of the door into the kitchen. Noting that the printer was warming up, he leant against it with his arms crossed and leant around the wall calling in to the kitchen.

"Dixie, I reckon we've got something here."

Dixie walked towards him, both cups held tightly, steaming.

"There you go mate," he said and handed Colin his mug.

Reaching down, he picked up the two sheets he had printed and walked back with Dixie to his desk.

As his mate sat down, Colin dropped the two intel sheets down in front of him.

"Have a look at these."

Dixie took a sip and quickly scanned the papers in front of him. Looking up to Colin he waved the two sheets.

"Reckon that is our man; only thing is both bits of intel are from unknown sources. I do not know whether the bosses will look at it the same way. Only one way to find out."

Colin nodded took the paperwork and walked towards the desk at the end of the room.

The Senior Investigating Officer, Inspector Ivor Dare, was sat hunched over several aerial photos, head in hands, studiously looking at the murder scene and surrounding areas. These had been taken by the Force's helicopter 24hrs after the incident. It was a clever way to refresh one's memory or brief someone.

Colin stood at the desk for about ten seconds before clearing his throat.

"Sir, sorry to trouble you."

Inspector Dare looked up.

"Sorry Colin, miles away; can I help?"

"Might be nothing boss, but then again, can you have a look at these two actions?"

Having passed them over, he crossed his arms and watched intently.

The experienced senior detective read one, then the other, and repeated it. Picking them up, he looked up at Colin, and stood up.

"I take it you've the noted the sources are untested, and low graded?"

Colin nodded. "Yes, but something keeps niggling at me, if you know what I mean."

The officer paused.

"OK let us take a punt, prioritise these. Create a new action linking them, and distribute for enquiry, asap."

Smiling Colin took them, said, "Thank you, boss," and strode back to his desk. As he passed his mate's desk, their eyes met, and he gave him the thumbs up. Sitting down he started typing eagerly and with a purpose. Little did he know that he had set the wheels in motion for what was to be a turnaround during the investigation.

On an investigation such as this, teams were divided into pairs, as far as possible. This was done really to ensure nothing was missed, that it was done properly, and of course for officer safety.

Detectives Dave Pauls and Norman Grover had been partners on several major enquiries, and worked well together, it is almost as though each knew what the other was thinking—ideal in these circumstances and surroundings. They and their partners mixed socially, and the women also got on like a house on fire, often keeping each other company whilst their husbands worked another long, exhausting day.

Sharing a lift as they always did, the two arrived early the next day. Dave had driven this week, and the following week it would be Norman. Parking the car in the overflow car park, they walked into the rear of the station and into the Major Incident Room.

After a quick catch up on current affairs and general chat with the others, Norman went to the room's in-tray and sifted through the actions awaiting allocation.

He picked up a large A4 envelope addressed to the two of them. Bemused, he picked it up and joined Dave who was stirring the two cups of coffee he had just poured.

Norman took the hot brew made by his mate.

"Let's have a gander at this then," he said, waving the brown envelope. Sitting down at the circular briefing table he opened it a read what had been written.

To: DCs Pauls and Grover
From: MIR
Re: Actions D551 and D552
Please read both actions as above.
Intel from two sources suggest the same information.
TIE male known as Curnow
Obtain Fingerprints and DNA
Treat as Priority

Having read it Norman went to the pool car cabinet and got the keys to a Ford Mondeo Estate and sat back down opposite Dave.

"Intel on the back of this has suggested a pub where this chap might be mate; it's a shithole. I've been there before when policing the football once, the idiots used to gather there pre-match."

Norman nodded. "Yeah, I know, oh well, I'll get a DNA kit and some statement paper."

TIE is 'Trace, Interview and Eliminate', and is used on all majors to either prove or cut an individual after interview, generally at a home address or place of work.

On occasions the officers may take DNA or fingerprints to eliminate or link an individual or individuals.

Norman picked up a kit from the stationary store, and a fingerprint and DNA kit from an adjoining cupboard, signing a small folder where he recorded the unique reference numbers appertaining to the kit.

He left the office and joined Dave who was on his phone in the rear yard. It was early, but the weather was promising, and the forecast was fair all week. This went some way to making the relentless questioning and travel a little more bearable. On a good day, the pair could complete about four of these tasks depending on where they were geographically.

Dave stood in front of the row of cars, and held the key up, pressing the remote. There was an audible bleep and flashing of the indicators on a blue Mondeo, and they headed towards it. Dave eased himself into the driver's seat, and Norman went to the rear and opened the boot, placing the kits and paperwork in there, whilst mentally noting the other items in there, and how messy it was. He would mention it on their return.

Both had at some time served in the Plymouth docks area and knew it well, which negated the need for either a map or sat nav.

Leaving the back gate, they swung left and on towards Plymouth; it would take about forty-five minutes.

In its day, the area around the north of Plymouth had a terrible reputation, mainly because of the clashes at night between locals and visiting ships crews; occasionally, Royal Marines.

It had got so bad in the late seventies, and early eighties that it was almost a no-go area for the emergency services and was known as 'Swilly'. The houses were council houses built in the twenties and remained almost untouched for the next sixty years.

There were dozens of stories of riots, and battles between locals and police, that even amongst police officers were legendary. The kids of today were the grandchildren and great-grandchildren of the problem makers all those years ago and were still just as bad. Families continued with their reputations almost as badges of honour. New and assorted styles of policing had won over, with a policy of zero tolerance and targeted policing. The enemies now were addictions: drugs, and alcohol.

The houses, built for working class families, and dockers, fell into disrepair, as the docks laid off people, and contracts in the dockyards were lost.

Dave and Norm reached the outskirts of North Prospect in just under forty minutes and had spent most of the journey moaning about the police, and useless bureaucrats who hold the purse strings. The experienced detectives had seen the purse strings tighten. There were simple things like limited access to the stationary store, which was now continually locked, and whose key was held by the office manager. This had always been a useful source of textbooks, pens and pencils, for the kids' homework.

Expenses were becoming less obtainable, and everything had to be itemised and VAT removed, so one was always out of pocket. The worst of all was that in any overtime claim, you could get the first half, as it was "on the Queen."

The car parked quietly on the faded yellow lines, obscured by discarded plastic bags and leaf litter. Dave turned off the ignition and unclipped his seatbelt, letting out a long sigh as he stared out of the side window at the shithole of a street they were about to enter.

Norman swivelled in his seat letting the seatbelt buckle hit the window as it recoiled into the car's pillar.

Reaching out, he picked up the two A4 notebooks and wallet holding all their bits and pieces, currently sealed in tamper proof bags.

Without speaking they climbed out and slammed the doors and moved on to the pavement. Pointing down the road on their right Dave read the pub sign that hung still in the air: The Port Cullis.

Norman reached down and pulled up on the waistband of his trousers and Dave cleared his throat.

"Well, there it is. Come on."

Both stepped off in unconscious unison and reached the filthy front door in less than a minute. Taking the lead paperwork in hand Norman entered followed by Dave, who acknowledged the door being held open.

Inside they were greeted by the smell of beer-sodden floorboards and the distant sound of the duelling banjos playing through a set of large wall-mounted speakers, behind a raised area to the right of the long bar.

There was a large television screen over their left shoulders showing racing horses being moved into their positions, and current odds and prices scrolling along the bottom of the screen.

The bar was almost empty except for an old chap with his accompanying Zimmer frame, pint of Guinness, eating crisps, and another chap stood just in front of the screen ticket in hand, watching intently. Both officers leant on the bar, placed the paperwork down and took out their warrant card wallets.

The bartender was surprisingly well turned out, and shaven, aged about thirty, looking like maybe he was doing this for pocket money, as opposed to a full-time career.

"Good afternoon," he greeted them. "What can I do for you officers?"

Placing his wallet in his back pocket, Norman spoke first.

"Do you know a chap called Chris Curnow? There's no problem, it's just that we're supposed to meet him here." The bartenders looked up and called over to the man intently watching the race which was about to start.

"Chris, some people here want to speak to you."

Chris Curnow reluctantly turned to face the direction of the voice.

"Fuck," he whispered under his breath. He could see who they were, and he could almost smell them, or so he thought.

The two officers walked over towards the stationary figure and pulled out their cards again.

Norman looked at the dishevelled Curnow, as Dave spoke.

"Chris, my name's Dave. Can we sit somewhere quiet and private; we'd like to have a chat?"

Pointing to the door leading to the snug Chris walked on followed by the two detectives.

Chris sat at a table which faced the entrance, his back against a wall, and dragged an empty ashtray towards him. Dave sat in front and to his left with Norm on his right. It had been decided in the car some time ago that Norm would take the lead.

Curnow lit a cigarette that had been lodged behind his left ear and took a long drag as he eyed the two officers, who were busy sifting through a folder extracting paperwork and pens.

Both officers eyed Curnow, as he exhaled a large cloud of smoke into the space between them, Norman raised a closed fist to his mouth and stifled a cough.

Clearing his throat Dave palmed the paperwork, sat upright and began.

"Firstly, can I just confirm a few details?"

Curnow nodded and mumbled something which neither officer could hear clearly.

"You are Cristopher Curnow, of no fixed abode, as of six months ago, date of birth 09/02/1952, correct?"

Curnow leant forward, and slowly reached out, stubbing the unfinished cigarette in the overflowing ashtray. He leant back and folded his arms shrugging his shoulders.

"The very same; what can I do for you?"

Curnow's cockiness had already pissed Norman off, as it was obvious the man in front of him was trying to get the upper hand.

"Listen to me carefully, very carefully, as your next answer will dictate whether I embark on a personal crusade to fuck your life over from now on, do you understand?"

His outburst caught his mate by surprise and made the Plymothian gangster wannabe sit up.

Dropping his hands to his lap, he stuttered, "A-all right boss, all right, keep your hair on."

Norman knew, as did Dave, that they had the upper hand now, and Curnow had been put in his place. This was old school policemanship at its best. The very fact he had called him boss, had confirmed that he had been a guest of Her Majesty at some time, a fact they knew anyway.

"Let's start again shall we; I am not in the mood for smart arse comments, and all this cocky shit."

Norman turned to Dave, who smiled and pen in hand started the interview.

The officers fired questions at the humbled Plymouth drunk. Questions and repetition sorted the truth from fiction

After about half an hour Dave stood up and stretching, stifled a yawn. Curnow had chain smoked through the bombardment, and he felt as though he had got himself into a corner, from which he could not escape, and was worried that he had embarked on a slippery road of trouble.

Sitting down again, Dave flicked through the notes he had scribbled down. Norman had also made copious notes and they were both pleased.

Norman cleared his throat as Curnow reached for another cigarette, whilst his earlier one burnt to a finish in the overloaded ashtray.

The bartender approached them and addressed the table.

"Can I get you gentlemen anything, Janner?" The latter related to Curnow and was a generic phrase for someone born in Devon.

Curnow declined but looked as if he could do with a large stiff drink.

"No we are fine thanks," said Norman.

The questioning had started with the two detectives outlining the incident and asking if he knew about it. He said that he heard about it in the news but did not think anything more about it. When asked how he felt about when he had heard, he just shrugged it off saying he did not give it a second thought. The detectives noted how his eyes had stared at the floor when asked and he seemed vacant of any emotion, but it was a put on, and they knew they had him.

With the question still fresh in his brain Norman leant

forward.

"Chris, there are rumours about, that there are two London Pikeys here about who are using local drivers, and villains to help them, and your name has cropped up a few times."

Curnow looked up at the killer question and gulped, wringing his hands he looked left and right nervously.

"Who the fuck has said that then—"

Norman cut him short.

"You know we can't say, but there is more than one, and they are trusted, well-used sources."

"Chris, we are really not here to pull punches, and the evidence all points to you knowing more than you are saying at the moment." Dave pulled his chair closer and continued. "I know what these people are like, and capable of. I want you to help us, because now from where I'm sitting you are as guilty of the things they have done as if you have done it yourself, do you understand?"

Curnow inhaled deeply and closed his eyes; he wished he were in a different place, away from all this. He knew there was no way out: if he did not make the right decision now, he would be dead, as word would get out, and there would be no place to hide, anywhere.

"Do you know what you are asking me to do, do you really know?"

Norman and Dave had him, they worked on a hunch, and got it right. The feeling was immense, and even though neither spoke, they were thinking the same. Dave nudged his partner, as Curnow slumped forward with his head in his hands.

"Fuck, fuck, fuck, *fuck*!"

He stared at the floor, and felt a reassuring hand tap his shoulder lightly. It was Norman.

"Chris we can make sure you are safe; we know these people, and our army is bigger and better than theirs. You need to do the right thing now."

The barman had been diligently cleaning and stocking up and had not paid much attention to the huddled figures in the corner. He noted Curnow looked ashen and had not drunk anything since the officers' arrival. As the three rose in unison and left, he reached under the till and opened a folded piece of paper. He turned to the black phone which was in its cradle on the wall. Picking it up he dialled the number carefully, and noting the time waited for an answer.

CHAPTER TWENTY-NINE

Curnow had been driven to the Enquiries Headquarters, by the detectives as quickly as possible. Dave's advanced driving training had kicked in the two seasoned coppers realised this was the breakthrough they had been looking for since they had hit all the brick walls that had faced them throughout the job. Both knew of all the jobs in the past that had been lost due to haste and not conducting the correct procedures, or forgetting the tiniest of detail, when excited or tired. It was not going to happen on their watch on this job.

Phone calls had been made en route in the car, which in turn had started the huge wheels within the enquiry.

Curnow was ready to tell all. He was tired of the relentless and never-ending dreary alcohol-sodden life he had led since a young boy in the ruins of war-ravaged Plymouth.

He was not loved and had no real friends. He was used to a life in the dark and working for just enough money to buy the next bottle. Norman and Dave, on telling the office of the impending arrival, and information which would be forthcoming, had been told to stand by, and await instructions.

The call came back quicker than the pair had expected, and it was answered just as quickly. The voice was slow and deliberate.

"I take it Curnow is in the car with you; if so, can he hear this conversation?" Norman looked to his left, at Curnow, who was slumped forward, with his hands over his ears, quietly sobbing, and for a moment, the officer felt a little sympathy. Norman paused and, changing the phone to his right ear. answered, "It's okay. Go ahead."

The instructions were deliberate and clear.

"Norman you Dave and Curnow, are to deviate and head to Exmouth Custody, so far?" Lowering the phone Norman leant forward and rested his chin on the back of the driver's seat, near Dave's right.

"Mate divert to Exmouth Custody suite, quick as you like." Leaning back and raising his phone Norman saw Dave's face in the rear-view mirror, and saw him silently mouth the new destination, with a quizzical expression, Norman nodded.

"Roger that. All received."

Curnow sat back in the seat, and wiping his eyes, cleared his throat.

"What's up?"

Ignoring him Norman remained listening to the conversation before hanging up and placing the mobile between his legs.

Norman addressed the puzzled Curnow.

"Chris, we are diverting to a safe location, where we can carry out a safe and legal interview, just relax and try and get a bit of kip."

Curnow slumped back and felt like a great weight had been taken from him; he closed his eyes, and for the first time in a very long time fell into a deep undisturbed sleep.

The car arrived at the police station in Exmouth, after about an hour and twenty minutes of trouble-free driving, down the A38, onto the Exeter to Exmouth A376. Traffic had been light, and that, combined with Dave's driving skill, made for substantial progress.

Entering the barrier to the left of the station, at the base of the small slope, the car paused. Winding the window down, Norman spoke into the intercom, as Dave leant over and shook Curnow, who woke with a start and look of bewilderment—he had been away with the fairies. The car edged forward.

"Where are we?" asked the confused passenger as the car parked in a bay outside of the magistrates court, which was part of the police station but was surrounded by brick and wire in the rear compound.

Before he could get any answer, his door was open, and Normans hand appeared.

"Come on Chris let's get a hot drink and something to eat." As he got out, Dave exited the car on the other side and striding over to a side door in the nick, pressed the intercom, and waited.

Curnow and the other officer and walked over to join him, as there was a loud click and the door opened inwards.

Inside there was a flurry of movement, and a uniformed sergeant and a civilian detention officer greeted the group.

"Mr Curnow, can you just go with this officer, and he'll get you food and drink, while I speak with the two officers." The burly shaven-headed detention officer took Curnow's arm gently.

"Come on chap, let us see what we have then."

As they disappeared out of view, the two detectives went with the sergeant into the custody centre, which was empty, and closed the door behind them.

In the main reception area, the custody sergeant took his place behind the bank of computers, which were atop the wooden desk. The whole area was raised, so that the custody staff looked down on whoever was being presented, but also acted as a barrier. The large desk-to-ceiling impact glass gave added protection, a sign of the violent times, or potential for violent prisoners.

The three sat down behind the counter.

Norman started.

"Sergeant, as you know we have visited Curnow in Plymouth, and it is obvious he wants to pass on vital information, and probably a lot more than were expecting."

The seasoned custody sergeant shuffled and held up his hand.

"I've had a brief from the senior investigating officer; Curnow is to be moved to a safe house, once armed response teams have turned up. I believe the house is in Lympstone Village. We don't want our suspects getting a whiff of where he is."

Norman turned to his mate and smiled.

"If it's okay we'll grab a bite and start getting things going; I take it he's incommunicado?"

The sergeant confirmed that he had no access to any forms of communication, nor did he have a phone on him.

CHAPTER THIRTY

Thomas and Michael Burns were on the drive of the farmhouse on the edge of Haytor, about five miles outside of Bovey Tracey, looking at the exposed engine of the Range Rover in front of them.

"Fucking shit, shit!" Michael shouted, as he slammed the bonnet down, narrowly missing his bigger brother's head and fingers. Throwing himself backwards, Thomas glared at his embarrassed brother.

"You twat, that nearly had my head; what the fuck is wrong with you?"

The awkward silence was broken by the soundtrack of *Apocalypse Now*, which was Thomas's ringtone on his phone. Maintaining his stare at his brother who had extended his arms in a 'what have I done wrong' type gesture, he pressed the answer button and spoke.

"What the fuck do you want? it had better be good."

Thomas leant against the car's wing, his left hand running along the bonnet as he listened intently.

"Well, where have they gone?" He stood up and looked at his brother. Michael went to say something, and Thomas held up his hand, stopping him before he could form a sentence, whilst listening intently to the voice on the other end of the phone. Michael moved closer, as Thomas nodded, and dropping the phone down so he could look at the screen, he thumbed the 'call end' button.

"Well, what the fuck was all that about?" asked the quizzical brother, as he stared at the face with the gaping mouth. Clearing his throat Thomas spoke.

"That spineless fuck Curnow, has spilt his bollocks to the filth."

Michael's brow tightened, as he tried to understand what this was all about. He was confused.

"Come again?"

Thomas shook the phone in the air.

"Curnow has gone to the cops!" His voice was raised and as he shouted, he showered his brother with spittle.

Michael replied, "Go on then, what's happened?"

Thomas relayed that day's events in Plymouth to his disbelieving brother. When he had finished the younger brother looked up into the air.

"He's a fucking dead man walking, the bastard."

Thomas nodded. "We're going to have to move our arses out of here soonest, else his new mates will come a-knocking."

The brothers strode silently into the rear door of the whitewashed farmhouse, and slammed the door shut behind them.

CHAPTER THIRTY-ONE

The house in Lympstone was in the estate that was used by the Royal Marines, generally those who are married with kids. This detached house, had been vacated by a captain who upon promotion had moved lock stock and barrel to 45 Commando in Arbroath Scotland, taking his young wife and two daughters with him.

A member of the team still had contacts with the Works Liaison Officer in the Royal Marines, who were responsible for billeting. A promise of a beer or two and a curry, had secured the use of this 'safehouse' for two weeks, until it had to be released and a new family housed.

Neighbours, also in the armed forces, were used to peculiar goings-on and would not think anything about the new temporary neighbours arriving and departing in vehicles with blacked-out windows.

Curnow had been debriefed and interviewed for over six hours at the police station before eventually being taken to the three bedroomed house, and now it was dusk.

His journey had been quiet, with no one saying anything. Norman and Dave had disappeared some time ago, and the normally mouthy Plymothian had been interviewed by two teams of experienced detectives. They had asked a myriad of questions about everything: his upbringing, associates, criminal life, vehicles, on and on, relentless. More importantly the two Traveller brothers, and what they had been up to.

Curnow was scared, really scared and it showed.

He had told them willingly everything he knew. How he had come to meet them initially, where he had been with them, what he had done, and confirming times and dates.

Most importantly he spoke about the day he drove them and others down to Wadebridge.

The Traveller brothers were interested in the isolated properties in the rural areas of South Devon. The now crumpled and humbled Devon alcoholic spoke in detail about the brothers and the Wadebridge job, and how he had started it with a simple harmless phone call.

Their crime spree had started years ago in the leafy suburbs of rural Kent and other locations fed by the easily accessible M25: places such as Saint Albans in Hertfordshire, and further afield, West Sussex via the M23, both proved to be rich pickings.

As they travelled, they found that the rich pickings also attracted other individuals and gangs like them, so the obvious targets had either been done or were about to be done. The plethora of attracted criminals in turn bought with them the police and private security firms.

When the brothers had received the call, they were sat in a pub near Colney Heath, The Billet. They had been scouring the local area for potential opportunities with a driver, in a black Nissan pickup, and were on their way home, but had stopped for a beer in the beer garden. They had made the driver, a Romanian, stay in the cab, whilst they ordered food at the bar, and took their seats in the sunny garden.

Thomas answered the phone with a sigh.

"I told you not to bother us; it had better be good." Placing it on loudspeaker, he placed it on the table between them, and looking around to see the other tables empty, hunched over and spoke. "You're on speaker, speak!"

Curnow cleared his throat.

"I've just seen a bit on the box, about a couple of rich artist types of girls who have moved down to a place called Wadebridge down here; they make really expensive furniture and the like."

Michael leant back, and placing his hands behind his neck, stretched, and looked at his brother, mouthing something. Thomas leaned closer to the phone.

"Please don't tell me you've rung us to give a commentary on what's on in fucking Devon, or I'll drive down there and superglue your fucking ears shut."

"No, no listen up," said the excited voice from Plymouth. "These girls are top-notch, big earners who were living and working in Chelsea, *Chelsea!* for fuck's sake. They've moved down here and are making this gear for all the top knobs all around the country. Imagine how much dosh they've got not to mention the gear in the house; it'll be a soft touch."

Michael leant forward and placed his elbows on the table and covered the phone with his left hand.

"I fancy a trip to the sea; ain't got nothing to lose, we've got money in the bank. Get him to have a look and we could take a spin down that way for a month or so, rent somewhere. What do you think?"

Thomas paused and then pulling out a fag from the packet on the table, passed one to his brother and placed another in his mouth.

Michael looked at Thomas, as he heard the muffled voice from the phone asking if anyone could hear him. The elder brother lit his cigarette and held the lighter to his brother who inhaled deeply, holding the smoke in.

"Listen carefully. Go have a look at this place, sound it out; we could do with a change of scenery."

Michael let the smoke out slowly and smiled, rubbing his dirty hands together. It was Tuesday, and they would be down Saturday morning. Thomas killed the call and turned as the bartender walked up and presented them with the two beers, and a menu.

The next day, Curnow was on his way down from Plymouth on the A30 to Wadebridge. He did not know where to go but would head for any of the garages near there and they would point him in the right direction.

Wednesday travelling on the A30 to Cornwall's North Coast, was a leisurely drive in the dark blue Ford Transit. It took about an hour and twenty minutes, until he reached the first garage on the outskirts of the town. Pulling up on the forecourt, he climbed down and filled the tank up. He had thought of doing a runner but had decided against it after seeing the discreet CCTV in the roof of the canopy; besides, he thought, they would all be down this way soon for quite a while and couldn't risk being a wanted person.

He walked into the shop and the door sounded a small bell that hung over it, as he swung it open.

The middle-aged lady at the till looked up from her counter, where she was pricing the Snicker bars.

"Forty pounds of diesel my love?" she asked hand hovering over the till. Curnow handed the two notes to her.

"Don't suppose you know of a high-end furniture outfit down here do you? Came down from London?" he asked.

Taking the notes she typed in the price on the ageing till.

"Oh you mean the mother and daughter down the road? Nice stuff but out of my price range. Continue down about three miles, branch left and it's on your right about half a mile down."

Curnow declined a receipt and thanked her. As he left, he had decided this would not be a place to rob; besides, the lady was nice. He smiled to himself. Settling into the driver's seat, he slammed the door and reached down beside the handbrake, and grabbed the bottle of cheap whiskey that was tucked in.

He swiftly took a large gulp and winced as he swallowed. Placing the bottle between his legs on the seat, he started the van and moved from the forecourt, back on to the A30. The short journey took less than fifteen minutes, and he slowed the vehicle as the driveway drew nearer on the right. Passing it he checked in the rear-view mirror and glanced forward. He noted the road was clear and stooped at the entrance. Looking towards the buildings he noted the new four-wheel-drive vehicles and saw two ladies speaking to a male on the gravelled drive. He squinted and noted that one female was older than the other, and that the younger one was attractive. The man they were speaking to was holding a bicycle and had some sort of apron around his waist; they were all laughing.

Curnow gently pulled forward out of sight of the drive but on the same side, facing any oncoming traffic, although he had yet to see another vehicle. Mounting the grassy verge, he yanked on the handbrake hard, and turned the ignition off with his right hand as his left reached for the bottle between his legs. He felt slightly giddy as he had not eaten, and the whiskey was slowly taking effect. Holding the bottle on his knee, his mind drifted as he stared ahead stifling a yawn. He unscrewed the bottle top, letting it drop to the floor, as he raised the bottle to his awaiting lips. Closing his eyes, he took several large gulps, before taking a breath and placing the bottle back between his legs. Opening his eyes, it took several seconds before the 'mist' cleared, and colours began to fill his view. Momentarily he could not remember where he was or what he was doing, until he turned his head abruptly to look out of his side window, and saw Devon Bank, and buildings beyond it.

Curnow cleared his throat and placed the almost empty bottle lidless on the passenger seat, allowing the remaining cheap whiskey to soak the oily, stained passenger seat.

Reaching up with his hands, he turned the rear-facing mirror, towards him and leant forward, staring into the empty unshaven face that stared ack at him. Pursing his lips, he looked at his stained and toothless grin, and sat back.

The many sodden years of drink made him impervious to cleanliness, and in any case he did not really care. Sliding across the two seats, Curnow opened the passenger door with his left hand, and swinging his right leg across climbed out on to the road. As he did the whiskey bottle fell on to the road, and shattered into dozens of pieces, scattered in the dark pool of cheap alcohol.

Looking down he bit on his lower lip and slapped his thigh with his clenched fist.

"Fuck it," he mumbled, and rolled his eyes.

There would be no drink until he got home now.

Slamming the door shut he walked along the side of the parked van, using his extended left arm to steady himself, as he reached the rear, and approach to the gravelled drive ahead of him.

Looking around, he took in his surroundings. Remote and set on its own, the buildings had the appearance of having been worked on recently, with what appeared to be new roofs, and pillared approach to the drive.

Reaching the entrance, he saw that the three figures were

walking together into what appeared to be the shop, which was about fifty metres away in a straight line from the main road.

Swinging around into the gravelled drive, he noted the wooden plaque on a chain on the right-hand pillar: 'Shop open'. Adjusting his grubby collar, he walked towards the door. Mother, daughter and trusted handyman were deep in conversation, gathered around a large oval dining table, which was just inside the entrance when the door opened.

All three looked up and daughter spoke first.

"Hello, please come in have a look around, and there is anything we can help with just give me a shout."

The dishevelled figure of Curnow looked up and scanned all three.

"Okay just browsing," he answered in an almost unintelligible mumble, whilst placing both of his hands into his pockets. Daughter smiled, looked back down at the oval table and continued the conversation.

Curnow skirted around the large open plan room, trying to keep as far away as possible from the owners. The room was full of an assortment or furniture and wood-based items. Some had obviously been made from scratch, others appeared a lot older, but in beautiful condition.

One thing that they all had in common was the price. All were in their hundreds, some even had the letters POA, all handwritten beautifully in black ink on the small white price tabs.

Leaning down he picked up a price guide and product catalogue, and flicked through it quickly, noting the prices.

Stuffing the leaflet in his left-hand pocket, he turned and headed to the exit. As he approached the door he turned.

"Thanks, some lovely stuff here," looking at the three who were still in deep conversation.

Tilly raised her head. "You are welcome, have a nice day," and watched as the dishevelled man fumbled with the door handle, opened the door and left, leaving it to slam behind him.

Curnow walked up to the van and climbed in the passenger side door, stepping in the glass of the broken whiskey bottle as he did. Settling into the driver's seat he started the engine and looked back over his right shoulder towards the entrance to the shop. His mind was going through a myriad of scenarios and was trying to think straight despite the whiskey trying to take him in other directions. Reaching into his pocket he pulled out the brochure he had taken from the shop as he had left. Throwing it into the passenger footwell, he put the van in gear and screeched away, from the grassy verge and headed back to Plymouth.

The Burns brothers had received the call from Curnow later that night. It was difficult to understand exactly everything he was saying, so he was instructed to stay put in the pub, and they would join him.

At about ten o'clock, the old Blue Saab estate pulled into the back of the car park of the run-down Devonport pub, which was Curnow's second home. Thomas Burns puffed on his thin rolled-up cigarette as he swung the car around the empty and litter ridden rear yard. His brother had the passenger window down, and threw his McDonald's bag and empty contents out, followed by a loud belch. The lights picked up the solitary figure of Curnow at the rear exit, and as the car came to a halt he strolled over.

Opening the rear left door, he slid in and leant forward with his head between the brothers' seats. His breath was a mixture of alcohol and stale cigarettes, as he handed Thomas the brochure he had picked up.

Curnow spoke. "The place is on its own right beside the

main road, easy to get to, easy to leave."

Michael Burns belched again, spat out of the window, and turned to face the Plymothian.

"You fucking in-breed, we're not interested in an AA route map, get on with it."

Curnow swallowed hard.

"In that brochure you'll see for sort of gear they have there, isn't nothing less than three hundred quid, and there's a lot there with another zero on the end. Look in the leaflet."

Thomas passed the paperwork to his brother and quietly lit another fag.

Curnow felt nervous in the silence, and the open windows were letting the cold evening air into the previously warm interior.

Leaning back into the seats he could not hear what the two large figures were talking about, but after what seemed like ten minutes the leaflet came flying into his lap.

"Get rid of that," barked Thomas.

Curnow stuffed it back into the pocket as the brothers turned to face him.

Michael cleared his throat.

"We'll give it a crack. We'll do it on Sunday as the takings will still be there from the week before. Three staff, two are bitches, should be an easy earner." He turned and faced his brother who nodded. They told Curnow to get over to the brothers' rented property for the next Friday night, with overnight stuff, sober, so they could put the plan into action Thomas leant closer.

"Cut the drinking, you need a clear head. There's to be no fuck-ups. In, out. Scare the girls, rough the geezer up and fuck off, now get out, and keep your mouth shut."

CHAPTER THIRTY-TWO

Reuben's eyes opened, and he blinked, trying to focus as the fuzziness in his head cleared. His bed was warm, and he did not want to get up and about. Turning to his left he saw that Sarah was still sound asleep but faced towards him. Looking at her face, he smiled to himself, and thought about what they would do today, there was no rush for her to get up, and he would leave her be. Turning his head, he stared up at the ceiling. Retirement was everything everyone had said and more. His pension had gone into his bank account the week before, about six weeks after he had walked out of the office for the last time. There had been no party or piss-up, despite the lads on the team urging him to have one.

Reuben had thought hard about it, but it was just something he did not want to do. The end of the day, end of my job, simples. There had been comments made when he had decided to accept his Long Service and Conduct Police Medal, through recorded delivery. Normally people receiving this attend a plush event at the Headquarters, where either the Chief Constable or one of his deputies would give an exuberant speech and shake copious amounts of hands, and pat everyone on their backs. Fuck that.

The service had changed, and the job, that he had loved had changed dramatically. No respect, No job for life, and no enjoyment.

Turning to his right, he propped himself up on his elbows, and reached out with his right hand to pick his mobile phone up, to see the time: 0746hrs. He slumped back, and held the phone on his chest, peering at it. It is odd, he thought, that the days fade into the next as seamlessly as a knife through butter. The weeks fly by, and he felt an age was passing him by. Glancing at his phone again he gently slid his body to right, easing himself out of the bed, trying not to disturb Sarah.

The kitchen had been extended, one of the first things they had done upon retirement, and mornings were spent drinking coffee watching the news on the huge wall-mounted screen, and when it was warmer, having the five-panel bi-folding doors wide open.

As he waited at the kitchen's island, he found himself daydreaming about nothing, when the whistling of the kettle bought him back into the here and now. As he poured the water into the stained unwashed mug, he glanced over his left shoulder to where his mobile, which was on charge, rumbled on the worktop, as it was on vibrate. Looking down on the phone, black coffee in hand, he squinted to see that it had been a missed call from Simon. Simon? He wondered what his old mate wanted.

"Hello Reuben." Simon had answered the call within a few rings. "Hope I didn't wake you."

"No, I was just enjoying yet another day of doing sod all." There was a pause.

"Are you sat down, mucker?" Reuben quizzed him.

"What's wrong?"

"I take it you have not seen the news then." Reuben glanced up at the screen on the wall.

Sitting down on the silver bar stool, he placed his coffee down balancing his phone against it and put it on loudspeaker.

"I've got Sky News on now," he said as he pressed the remote. The phone went quiet, and Reuben said, "Ring you back" as he listened to the local reporter as he stood outside of Dartmoor Prison.

The reporter was dressed in a thick coat to protect him from the sideways slanting rain that was making his report more dramatic. Reuben watched and listened intently, motionless. After a short while the screen flicked to another article, and another reporter, and Reuben turned the TV off.

His mind was tumbling over what he had just heard. The Burns twins had won an appeal in the appeals court and their conviction had been quashed due to a re-examination of witness evidence given at the time. They were expected to be released imminently.

Reuben's phone jumped into life again, causing him to jump.

"Can't believe it!" he said to his mate.

Simon, who was still serving, had told him over the last months that the appeal was underway.

They discussed at length the case and their surprise at the appeal results. Neither of them would have dreamed, when they had arrested the brothers at gunpoint, that years later, they would be hearing that the two were to be released because of faulty evidence.

Reuben guessed that it was probably because of Curnow's evidence, and the fact that someone had got to him. The brothers undoubtedly had money behind them, as well as far-reaching heavy muscle.

Reuben was sat down in the extension, with the TV muted when Sarah walked in.

There was no reply to the "good morning" she muttered, and she continued pouring her coffee which Reuben had prepared earlier.

Sarah sat beside him, he had not budged or acknowledged

her at all.

"Er hello," she said, watching him as she spoke.

He jerked his head around from the muted screen on the wall.

"Sorry love, morning."

"Wrong side of the bed?"

He smiled leant across and kissed her forehead.

"No, I just been on the phone to one of the lads."

Pointing at the muted screen, he explained what the conversation had been about. Sarah listened intently, and to the following rant, full of profanities, which followed, unprompted.

Sarah knew what toll this whole job had taken on both Reuben and his team, the long, long hours and stress over many months.

She knew that this whole sorry sad tale would occupy Reuben's head for a long time now. She reached over and squeezed his hand as he continued his rant and protestations.

CHAPTER THIRTY-THREE

Since Reuben had retired, the team had changed quite a bit, and continued to be the spearhead in the fight against the very worst of the criminal fraternity. Over the next year or so, other team members also retired, to put their exhausted feet up and enjoy life with their fat pensions and families, if they had them.

Rick was one of them; he had been the other Method of Entry Officer alongside Reuben and Steve.

All had the big thickset physiques, and coincidentally had been Royal Marines. Dave was a gym monster, having got the appetite from when he was a physical training instructor in the Corps.

His bungalow in the East Devon countryside was detached, and neat, but big enough to suit him, his wife Sadie, and young son, Eric.

Sadie and Dave were salt and pepper, and one would never put them together, yet they suited each other; they do say opposites attract.

Since retiring, Rick had little contact with his colleagues from the team, apart from the odd phone call. He was still serving when the news broke about the twins and the appeal almost eighteen months ago now. But it had not bothered him to any great extent.

Every other day he would leave the training in the gym he had built in the garage and take the hour's walk into Exmouth to the small spit and sawdust gym that he had been a member of for over five years.

Today it was a fine day, with clear blue skies and the house was empty. Being a Tuesday Sadie had gone to a friends for brunch, having dropped Eric at his school which was not a million miles away from the gym near Exmouth's sea front, so he decided to walk down to the local sea front in Lympstone, via the back lanes, it would only take ten minutes or so at a leisurely pace.

Wearing his old blue, Exmouth Rugby Club shorts, and Weird Fish jumper, he slid on some old trainers, and locking the door behind him, walked down the short drive towards the main gate.

As he got to the junction of the roads, he realised he had left his phone in the house. He hesitated and tapped his pockets.

Yes, it had been left in the house. Pausing, he turned and walked into the road, cursing and noticed the two as he did, he did not need it. Turning left he headed towards the wooden kissing gate, and signposted bridle path which was the shortest route to the small beachfront and welcoming coffee shop. He hadn't noticed the Vauxhall Insignia estate, parked a short distance away; why should he have?

Closing then gate behind him, he placed his hands in his pockets and turned on to the well-worn path lined on both sides with well-kept trees and bushes. The smell of wild onion was almost overpowering but pleasant, and reminded him of his childhood days, over forty years ago in Hampshire.

As he walked, he looked around him taking in the sights and sounds and noticed the two men walking slowly in front of him, in the same direction. He winced slightly as he caught the whiff of body odour, and what he thought was alcohol. Rick wanted to pass these two and the uncomfortable smell. Speeding up he took his hands out his pockets and approached the two, moving to their left as he said, "Excuse me, gents."

The two moved over the right without uttering a word. Turning slightly, Rick squeezed past, being careful not to brush up against the left-hand man.

The man's left forearm raised and swung back before he knew what was happening, hitting him hard across his neck. The force knocked him back and he fell to the ground, unable to catch his breath or stop himself from falling. As he struck the ground, something hit him hard across the side of his head, and a dark cloud enveloped him. As he had fallen, the nearest male had delivered a savage football-style kick to the side of his head, followed immediately by a ferocious heel stamp across the bridge of his nose. Dave's breathing was laboured and gurgled with the blood that was filling his airwaves and spilling on to his pale grey top. There were no defensive movements or attempts to get up. There never would be, the two kicks had made sure of that. The two unknown assailants stood over the still figure of their victim. The second male reached into his right trouser pocket and with a gloved hand took out the sharpened stick, which fitted nicely inside his clenched fist. Kneeling he pushed the sharpened end into the corner of Dave's right eye, which was closed, so that it was upright in the eyes' socket. Standing up, he raised his foot and stamped down hard. The laboured breathing and gurgling stopped immediately.

Thomas Burns turned to his brother who had lit a cigarette and had been watching the track.

"Like a stuck pig," he whispered. They giggled. Stepping over the still figure, they walked back towards the kissing gate and waiting car.

CHAPTER THIRTY-FOUR

Reuben had had a lazy day. He and Sarah had mooched about most of the day, and he caught up on all the emails that had accumulated over the last couple of days. Mid-morning, he had made himself some crackers and strong cheese washed down with a hot mug of white coffee; this more than made up for not having porridge for breakfast. Sarah had declined his kind offer to share it opting to refrain until lunch later.

He must have nodded off, because he jolted up in his chair in the extension, as his mobile phone rang out. Clearing his throat, he sighed as he just managed to catch the small plate as it slid from his knee. The phone stopped, and he placed the empty saucer on the table beside the still warm mug. Squinting at the phone he saw that it was past twelve.

Blimey, he thought. *I must have dozed off for more than thirty minutes.* He also noted that the call he had missed was from Steve, his old mate from the team. Reuben screwed his eyes up. *He never rings,* he thought.

He called the number back, placed the phone up to his ear and settled back in the comfortable winged chair, crossing his legs. The phone only rang a couple of times, and Reuben immediately recognised the soft dulcet Irish tones of Steve's voice.

"Reuben, sorry to bother you. Have you heard from any of the boys today?"

Reuben said that he hadn't and asked why.

"Mate it's not good; it's really bad shit. Rick's been found dead near his home, looks like someone's done him in. Colleagues say it was really bad as well."

Reuben was stunned, and words would not form, he stuttered out words that made no sense at first.

"What? When? Was he alone?"

The questions poured out; Steve stopped him.

"Reuben, all I know is that it looks like he's either come across something, or he has been deliberately attacked, but it's bad, very bad. Police are round his house now. Thought I'd let you know but I've got to go now. Stay near your phone and I'll get an update and ring you as soon as I know anything."

Reuben didn't say anything he just lowered his phone down on to the table and stared at the wall in front of him. His head spun with images and questions. Dave had been a great friend and even better colleague. An extraordinarily strong dependable mate, who loved his family and the life he had made for himself. Who would have done this, he wondered?

Sarah entered the kitchen from the stairs, dusting cloth and polish in hand.

"You all right love?" she asked.

Reuben looked up, ashen faced, his eyes welling up.

"Rick's dead, Sarah, they found his body near his house. Steve is saying he has been murdered! I cannot believe it, Rick, my mate."

Sarah went over to Reuben whose head was in his hands, and knelt beside him, she held him as he sobbed, and she cried too.

That day seemed to go on forever; tears were shed, and questions were asked but there were no answers.

Sarah had arranged to go and see Dave's wife later, as they were almost best girlfriends.

Reuben had been in touch with all the old team, and everyone was able to add a little more until a fuller picture was put together. The press and media had got the information almost at once, and the first report was on local radio and on the Internet via Devon Live.

Later that evening, Reuben felt drained and was not keen on letting Sarah drive off to see Rick's family but knew that the two ladies had had a long and tearful telephone conversation, and apart from her son, his wife had no one down here to turn to.

As Sarah pulled away, Reuben went back into the house and into the back garden, where he sat on the swinging seat beside the shed, that he was converting into a man cave. Gently swinging in the warm evening air, he turned things over in his mind.

The information that came in from contacts he still knew in the police did not offer much hope, but one thing he did know is that Dave did not make enemies, or attract unwanted attention, he had been just a nice guy, the best.

They had worked together for many years, and been in some bad shit, work wise, but always came out the other side.

The road behind the house was a rat run for the locals, and Reuben knew most of the people nearby, and vehicles they drove. The hedge at the bottom of the garden was sparse and functioned as a light wind break, besides which, Reuben and Sarah kept on top of it by regularly cutting it back, exposing the wild strawberry plants in the summer, and the blackberry brambles, both of which they picked when they were able to.

The swing chair faced the hedgerow, and the pair of them would often sit on the garden furniture watching the world go by, reading with a glass of wine, or just relaxing.

Reuben was miles away, turning things over when

something snapped back into the here and now.

His vision sharpened, and he stopped the swinging motion. Over to his left, in front of him were the dark shapes of two people, who appeared to be standing still looking through the hedge into his garden. Standing up he squinted and leant forward for a better view. As he did the figures melted away, moving out of sight.

There was a small gate about ten metres away that gave access to the road. He walked towards it, opened it and looked left down the road. He saw two people, in dark casual clothing approaching a car that was parked up. They got into the two front seats. It was too far away to get a registration number, but it just seemed a little odd, perhaps he was thinking too much. The car pulled away and drove down the lane until it disappeared out of view. Reuben watched for a couple of seconds then turned to go back to the house. As he opened the gate, he paused. Something did not seem right, call it a copper's nose, or gut feeling, whatever, but the hairs were standing up all over and he didn't know why. Entering the house, he went into the kitchen and picking up his phone rang Sarah. She was still driving but answered her phone. He sighed and told her to be careful, he loved her, and he would see her soon.

Sitting down he lay his legs on the pouffe and drifted off into a troublesome and probing sleep.

CHAPTER THIRTY-FIVE

People often say that they would like to attend their own funerals, to see who turned up and who said what about them. Three months after the coroner released Rick's body, the funeral took place at Lympstone Parish Church. If Rick had been able to see it, he would have been proud. People had travelled far and wide to see him off. The speeches at the church had been moving and beautiful. Reuben had prepared a speech but was unable to deliver it; he hoped his mate would have understood.

All the remining members of the old team were there and were collective in their visible grief. As a team they had seen and experienced things that would and should never be forgotten. As with all small elite teams such as this, your colleagues become your surrogate family, and sometimes you spend more time with them than you do with your families at home. A loss is as dramatic as losing a loved one, and they in their own ways loved each other. They all sobbed as Rick arrived in the hearse, with his wife and son following, supported by Reuben's wife. Each had accepted the privilege of carrying their colleague into the service and to his final resting place. The day was long, and exhausting, both physically and emotionally.

The wake was a small affair, with invited guests only, due to the massive response and attendance. It was in the function room of one of the numerous little pubs that were in and around Lympstone and a favourite of Rick's. As people drifted off the team remained in the small back room talking and laughing at length at the antics they had all got up to. Their partners and wives had left some time ago to go back to the house to comfort his wife Sadie, and his son Eric, who was terribly upset.

Reuben set the tray down with the assorted drinks, and eager hands reached out to take the drinks. Phil stood up and moved his chair back.

"A toast, gentlemen!"

In unison the team, once again together, stood and extended their drinks.

"To Rick, a hero, and a gentleman. God bless."

They all sipped from their glasses and sat. Jason was the first to speak.

"What I don't get is why the extreme violence; if it was a mugging, then why Rick, why sleepy Lympstone? There has been no intel about sus people or any crime wave pattern of note, so why?"

Tim, who had been quiet for a while cleared his throat.

"I think he was targeted."

All eyes turned towards him in an awkward silence.

"You're all thinking the same, the same as me. I think it was done to send a message, a punishment."

Brian spoke, his voice was raised.

"Fuck me! Steady on, Tim, we don't all think that!"

Phil shuffled forward on his seat.

"The enquiry has also come to that scenario, but as we know Rick was so black and white; they even looked into whether maybe he had strayed in the marriage for fuck's sake, a suggestion we all know is bollocks."

Jason then said something that killed the conversation.

"I even think it's something we have done as a team; I'm looking over my shoulder all the time, and looking at everything in a different way, wondering if maybe me or my family are next. Silly, I know."

There was silence for what seemed a long time until Reuben spoke.

"Jason it's not just you. I saw something…" and stopped himself from saying anything else by raising his glass to his lips.

"Go on Reuben, continue," said his mate.

"No it's probably nothing," said Reuben looking slightly sheepish.

"Go on," said Phil.

Reuben hesitantly mentioned the two men he noted on the evening of Rick's death.

Phil stood up and raised his hand.

"Right, come on now lad's, there's nothing going on here, team wise; there's no conspiracy, or vendetta, or whatever." Reuben looked at the seated group and shrugged with a grin, that widened into a smile. They all raised their glasses and put any ideas that they had to bed.

CHAPTER THIRTY-SIX

Rick's death seemed like a distant memory although it had been only six months. The enquiry was still ongoing but was no further forward. The general feeling was that it would go unsolved,

It was sad that everything outside of that continued as normal, but it did.

Reuben still had a nagging annoying feeling about the death and his encounter that same day. He had spent hours and hours thinking things over, turning it over in his head, fuelled by Jason's comment at the wake.

Sarah had kept a close eye on Rick's widow and had ensured that she always had someone to speak to, and the police network had also been good to her. Sarah had told Reuben that she felt the grieving widow would sell up and move away to be with her family in Kent. Rick's pension, and the sale of the house would be enough to help her relocate if it were the case, and she would be missed.

It was Thursday morning, and Sarah had gone to Sadie's and was expected to have a girlies' night, with a stopover, returning later on Friday.

All the chores had been done, and Reuben had settled into the chair in the extension. Laptop on his lap, he was looking into the possibility of buying a classic car, to renovate as a hobby, nothing expensive or to complicated, maybe an old Triumph Spitfire or similar. He had set himself a buying limit of about three and a half thousand pounds. His research had suggested he would be able to get one that needed work but would be within the ability of a DIY type person as opposed to a true enthusiast. The small, detached garage should be more than suitable enough, he thought, and a project would stop him getting bored, and keep him out of mischief.

His phone started ringing on the small coffee table beside him. Glancing down he could see that the caller ID was Wifey. Answering it, he was met with a rush of words, which he could not understand.

"Calm down, calm down love, what's wrong, where are you?"

"Reuben, you have to come here, quickly, please! I'm scared, really scared!"

Reuben stood up. "Where are you now? What's happened?"

"Two men spoke to me on the petrol forecourt; they know you; they told me... oh Reuben!"

Sarah sobbed on the phone, and he knew he had to be there. She was at the petrol station, and Reuben had confirmed they were gone. Telling her to wait in the shop on the forecourt, he ran out of the house grabbing car keys and coat, and raced to the station, only a short drive away. It felt that the journey went on for ages. Sarah did not scare easily, and she sounded frightened. Reuben was turning so many things over in his mind: what had happened? In fact, he arrived in less than ten minutes, and he had thrashed the car in every gear, without even knowing it. Pulling on to the forecourt he could see Sarah's car at the pumps, and her figure by the counter in the shop. Parking in a bay at the front of the door, he stepped out and momentarily looked around him. The forecourt was empty. Closing and locking the door he walked to the entrance as Sarah left and ran into his outstretched arms.

Reuben held her tight.

"It's all right love I'm here now, it's all right. What's happened?"

Sarah looked up at him.

"I was just about to fill up, when a car pulled up alongside me. At first I didn't notice anything, but it was odd because no one got out."

"Go on," said Reuben.

"The passenger window wound down, and I noticed that the man was looking at me, and he was smoking. I just smiled and said something like 'I don't think it's a good idea to be smoking with all this petrol about'. He just stared, and puffed away on it, and said something which I couldn't hear very well, so I said 'Pardon?' With that the driver opened his door and stood up, quickly. He said, 'You watch your mouth, or we will light you up'." Sarah gulped and continued. "The passenger was going to get out, when the cashier spoke on the tannoy: 'No smoking on the forecourt, please extinguish your cigarette'. It was then the that the driver leant into the car and shouted at the passenger with the cigarette, 'You stupid twat'. The driver got back into the car, and they were shouting at each other, As they went to pull away, the man nearest me formed his left hand into the shape of a gun, pointed it at me and said 'bang!'. They then tore off, on to the main road."

Reuben hugged Sarah. She was shaking, and visibly upset. They walked back into the shop, and up to the counter. The young lady at the counter had seen what had happened but could not hear what was said.

She looked at Sarah and Reuben.

"I have that on video; what on earth started all that?" Reuben looked at the CCTV camera above the cashier, and then out on to

221

the forecourt through the window.

"Could you do me a favour, can you rewind the video for me?"

The girl paused looking at the figure of Sarah, clutching Reuben and burying her head into his chest.

"I can do; it's got no sound, but the images are surprisingly good. I can bring the footage up on here," pointing to a computer monitor on her desk.

"I just need to see the car, registration number, and images of the two blokes," said Reuben. Turning the monitor slightly. Reuben leant forward leaning on the pile of free newspapers, which were complimentary with every purchase. Sarah wiped her nose and let go of Reuben, enabling him to get a clearer picture. The cashier was thankful that the garage was quiet, as she rewound the images and let the strangers look. She knew that she shouldn't really have, but the incident and image of Sarah who was hysterical, overrode the legal implications.

Reuben's eyes widened as the images were played back, and there was a lightbulb moment. He swallowed hard.

"Thank you, my love, you've been a great help. Can I ask one more favour, can I leave Sarah's car here? I'll park it up and pick it up later."

The cashier agreed and showed Rueben where it would be safe until later. Parking the car and taking Sarah to his only took a few minutes, and they were soon on their way. As he drove, he kept his worrying thought to himself, doubting that he was right, surely not. The drive home seemed to last for a long time, and Reuben was worried.

Once home, he had made Sarah a nice cup of tea, and he pampered her, as he knew the whole incident had upset her. Suggesting she lie down for a while in the spare bedroom, he kissed her gently on the forehead, and gave her a tight squeeze. He watched as the bedroom door closed behind her.

Taking his tea, he went into the study and drew his chair up at the small writing desk.

He mulled over the morning's events and jotted down the car's registration number on the pad in front of him. Taking a long sip of tea, he underlined the registration number several times.

He knew where he had seen the car before, and he was adamant that the car and the occupants were the same as the car that he had seen in the back lane only a couple of days ago. Picking up the phone he rang Pete, his old skipper at Police Headquarters. The phone was answered almost at once.

"Pete it's Reuben; I have a massive favour to ask, mate."

There was a pause.

"I'm all ears mate."

Reuben started talking and his old boss listened.

Sarah slept soundly and Reuben was left to mull over what Pete had said. He should not have passed the information really, but all the team kept in touch, and both knew the importance of getting to the bottom of what had happened to Sarah.

The pad in front of him had numbers, names, doodles, and etchings of nothing. Central to this was the registration number, which was false, and related to nothing, nothing or no one.

Reuben placed the pen down and leant back in his chair. The policeman in him was tumbling things over and over.

Rick's death had weighed heavily on all those who knew him, more especially since there was no clear motive. What nagged him was comment about it not being as straightforward as it seemed; what if it was a deliberate attempt on the team?

He shuddered as he wondered whether the sighting of the car

in the lane behind his house was an interruption of something more sinister.

    Reuben picked up his phone and decided to ring all the team that he had once been a proud member of. He would tell them what had happened and give them a heads-up, warn them to keep their wits about them, and just see what they thought.

CHAPTER THIRTY-SEVEN

Jason had stayed on the team right up to the last minute, much like Reuben. He too had genuinely believed it had been the best fifteen years of his thirty years in the Force.

He had remained single, enjoying his life, doing what he wanted to do with whomever he wanted to be with and wherever he wanted to be. His newfound love of 'gawking' had overtaken everything, and he was out most days in all weathers. Metal Detectorists, as everyone would normally know them to be, were by and large a resilient weatherproof bunch, and Steve was no exception. It was a relatively inexpensive hobby apart from the initial outlay, and his pension lump sum had hardly been touched.

The last time he had seen any of the lads was at the funeral, and it had upset him a great deal, although he hid his emotions well. On his return home that day he had sobbed as soon as he had stepped into the front door.

Over the last week or so he had been researching his latest interest, where he intended to search. Upon his dining table he had a plethora of paperwork, maps, and books open at salient pages concerning the area of Heathfield just off the A38 near Newton Abbot, what is now a massive industrial estate.

As you approach it from any direction you are signposted by the tall tower of what was Candy Tiles, an industry that employed many from the surrounding areas. The tall plume of steam from the ovens now extinct since it went into receivership.

In the later stages of the Second World War, the estate had

been the base for the American army, and it was a massive planning area which based and housed a considerable number of service members, and an even larger number of ammunitions and equipment. Rumour has it that towards the end of the war tons and tons of it were buried on site before the Yanks left to go into Europe, and the end of the war.

There are even new Harley Davidson motorcycles in greaseproof wrapping, apparently, as well as other larger vehicles.

The more he investigated it the more excited he got, but getting information from proper military sources was not possible, as it was still top secret, for some reason. Most of his info came from books, papers, and locals.

He had tried hard to determine who you had to speak to obtain permission to be able to walk around detecting, and hopefully, unearthing.

Jason was not one to buck the system, and trample all over private property, but the urge to get there and have a rummage overpowered any sensible thoughts and legalities.

He was happy that he had found the ideal place to start, and a drive the previous day had revealed that he could gain access by initially parking up opposite the newly built Marks and Spencer's garage in the entrance to the woodlands, like several dog walkers do, and hopefully melt away into the woodlands, equipment in hand, and start his searching.

Amongst the paperwork on his desk was his trusty Filofax, a throwback from the time when it was a must if you had a busy and/or hectic work life. When he was on the teams it was the subject of a lot of piss-taking and jibbing with the persistent question of 'why not get a good phone or manage your life better?'. He ignored it all and left them to it. Today had been a long day, and he had done lots of finalisation, before the following morning. As it was a Tuesday, he hoped it would be quiet, and that he would be able to melt away amongst all the walkers and dog walkers.

Standing up he stretched and let out a long yawn. Bending down he turned the table light off and pushed the chair in. Tomorrow would be another long day, but he was looking forward to it.

He awoke, after a troublesome and topsy-turvy sleep; he often did not sleep well if he had things on his mind and last night was no different. There was a slight apprehension in what he was going to do, but also excitement. Climbing out of bed he put on his dressing down and having paid a visit to the toilet, went downstairs to the lounge. As he got to the bottom of the stairs, he was stopped in his tracks by a sudden feeing of chilly air that swept over him. Looking over to the study, he noticed the thin blue curtains which were slightly open, blowing in an invisible air flow. He was curious, and he walked over and opened the curtains, to find the sliding doors open, only a little but open nonetheless.

If Jason was anything, he was methodical and mechanical in his routines, and it was odd to find the doors open. Pulling the doors open he stepped out and turned to look at the doors from the outside. As he peered carefully, he actioned the handles, and watched as the lock struggled to work properly. Feeling the framework around the lock revealed a roughness, which was unusual. Something had been used to force the lock from the outside, and he stood up and quickly looked around himself. Something was not right; there was an uneasy feeling. Entering the house, he pulled the door to, feeling it grind as he pulled the handles up engaging the damaged locking mechanism.

With his back against the door, he looked around. Someone had been in, he knew it. The papers on the desk had been moved, only slightly but moved nonetheless. Nothing appeared to have been taken, and he walked over to the desk, which had been lit up by the morning rays of sun now streaming in since the curtains were open.

Peering down he could see his Filofax had been moved, and the page marker was lying to one side.

A half-hour search of his house could not reveal that anything had been taken; nothing else had been disturbed. Odd, he thought.

Jason sat down and rung the promulgated 101 non-emergency number, to report the burglary. The police would not be attending; he knew that they would say that, but he thought he should have called, as it may be one of a few in the area, or a series.

Once he had made the call, he washed, dressed, and loaded the car. This time he left by the front door, and left the rear doors locked, with one of the wooden chairs pulled up against them, just in case. *It was just an opportunist,* he thought. His fault: he should not have left things on show, schoolchild error.

He had parked the car in the drive nose in, and as careful as he was, he would not have seen the grey coloured Vauxhall Insignia, parked approximately fifty metres away. Jason pulled out onto the road, and he turned the radio on, and headed off towards Heathfield, a journey of about thirty minutes. As he turned the corner at the end of the road, the grey car pulled away, a short distance behind.

The journey to Heathfield was uneventful, and traffic was light. Moving into the small lane was easy enough, with no other walkers, or dog owners already in situ.

He decided to park his car with the tailgate tight up against the fence to hopefully negate another enterprising person from taking any of his stuff, although he would take most of it with him.

Having reversed the car in as tight as possible, he leant over the seat and bought all his gear over and out of the driver's seat onto the floor. Apart from the main detector, most of the equipment was kept in one large North Face bergen, a legacy of his time on the Firearms team; it was an item that every member had been issued.

He had decided to keep the detector folded, to ensure no one would be suspicious and picking up the bergen, approached the large wooden gate with kissing gate turnstile.

The gate closed with a bang behind him, and he paused, glancing down at the watch which displayed not only a digital compass but also a route which had been inputted by him the night before. Glancing up and turning slightly, he decided on the best route and started to walk off into the woods. When he had been a Royal Marine all these years ago, they had all been taught to record their own paces to 100 metres; his had been 100. The purpose of this is that you would be able to accurately walk in a particular direction at night or in inclement weather to within a metre or so of your destination over considerable distances. The route into the woods was almost a straight line. He began walking and counted down silently in his head.

It might have been this that took his concentration away from the view off to his right, as the two dark figures entered the thicket in front of him.

The route was easy and unobstructed, just requiring ducking down, or pushing branches to one side, occasionally looking down at the watch on his arm.

He reached the point which had been punched into the route finder. Proud with himself, he smiled and was excited at the thought of the explorations ahead of him.

He unslung the packed backpack, and dropped to one knee, placing the bag in front of him. As he pulled the flap open, a noise ahead of him stopped him and made him look up.

Squinting, he held his breath, and peered at the thick bush about five metres to his front. Something or someone was crouched down within the thicket.

"Hello!" Standing up he kept looking at the thicket when a figure stood up and stepped to its right, appearing from the foliage.

Jason estimated the figure whom he guessed to be male, was over six feet tall, and dressed in black from head to foot. His hands were hanging loosely at his side.

He did not sense the figure that approached silently from behind him nor feel the barrel of the silenced pistol as it was raised to the back of his head.

The first round struck the back of his skull, exiting his right cheekbone, in an explosion of brain matter and crushed bone. He was dead before the bullet struck the ground. The impact forced him back on his knees, onto his back facing up, staring at the figure that hunched over him, with dead eyes. The second male walked over to join the hunched figure, with another weapon in his hand.

As he got to the lifeless body, he fired the first of two rounds into the prone body.

Neither of the two figures spoke as they walked away to the kissing gate, and back to their grey car.

Less than five minutes later the car was screeching out of the entrance, and heading off towards Bovey Tracey, and Dartmoor beyond.

The lifeless body was found four hours later by a member of the local running club, who had gone for a jog with her inquisitive Labrador. Upon her phone call, it was less than half an hour before the area was cordoned off and police were in attendance.

Reuben was tucked up in bed having been out with Sarah, in Exeter, earlier. Shopping had always been the most horrendous things that he had to do with Sarah. Upon his return he had sipped a large brandy, and settled in front of the radio, listening to Steve Wright in the afternoon. Sarah had retreated to the bedroom laden down with bags, and collapsed on the bed. He dropped into a quick and deep sleep, hurled back to his Commando days, in Hong Kong for some reason. Hedonistic, fun-filled but hard days, with great colleagues, making exceptional stories, which would be recounted years later.

The continuous sound of his phone vibrating slowly woke him up and begrudgingly he reached out eyes closed and answered it whilst wiping the saliva away from the one corner of his mouth.

The voice on the other end of the phone was Mick on the murder team, at Middlemoor Police Station.

The conversation that followed only lasted for about three minutes, then Reuben sat up and ended the call. His hand and phone rested on his lap, as he sat up, staring out of the window, scarcely believing what he had just heard. He dropped the phone to the floor and both hands came up to his face, and he sobbed, uncontrollably like a baby.

In the weeks that followed there was a lot of toing and froing, and phone calls, and team meets.

The unexpected and graphic murder was another that

appeared random, but Reuben knew differently, and the suspicions that had been raised prior to his death, regarding Rick's death, now held more credence.

Reuben had been going over the recent deaths of his friends in finite detail.

He was in a perfect position, where colleagues still serving were more than willing to pass on information, to which the media and public did not have access.

To him it was obvious that someone was out to deliberately murder the team that had been together for so long.

He had cleared his study in the neat bungalow in Lympstone, and drawn the curtains and blinds permanently, since the most recent death, much to the annoyance of his wife, Sarah, but she somehow understood. On the occasions she had looked in on Reuben when he had dozed off at his desk, in the dark room, she wondered at the mass of paperwork and files that he had surrounded himself with.

Although it did not appear so, it was organised chaos: he knew exactly what he was after, and he felt he had the answer.

CHAPTER THIRTY-EIGHT

Reuben had decided to keep all his suspicions to himself. He had deliberately not involved Sarah in any of his thoughts and intentions; the less said, the better.

He had decided what he had to do. It went beyond what is normal, it swept away all reasonable and sensible thought processes. It put Sarah's and his life in second place.

In his head he felt this wouldn't end, and that he could stop it now before more of the people he loved perished.

It was mid-morning, and Reuben and Sarah had enjoyed a quiet yet leisurely breakfast of toast and tea in the dining room.

"What are you up to today?" asked Sarah as she cleared the cutlery from the table, walking into the kitchen.

Reuben lied. "I thought I'd take a spin out to Woodbury Common and have a walk."

Sarah returned, hands on hip, with a wry smile across her face.

"I said I'd meet a couple of the girls and pop into Exeter, get my nails done, and have a bite to eat. Not expecting to rush back if that is okay?"

Reuben couldn't have played it better.

"That will be nice," and he smiled back. "Do we need anything whilst I'm out?" The negative reply from Sarah pleased him even more as he hated shopping with a vengeance. Woodbury was not his destination; his plan was morphing, and before he committed, he needed to get eyes on the premises on the edge of Bovey Tracey.

Sarah had left the driveway in her friend Karen's car, and slowly disappeared out of view as Reuben slid his walking shoes on and zipped up his Barbour Gillet. Karen and Sarah had known each other since school and remained friends ever since. They would be gone for most of the day.

Reuben left in his car shortly after and joined the A376 out of Exmouth towards Exeter, and the M5. He reached the turnoff to Bovey Tracey, in less than fifteen minutes, with light traffic, and no road works.

He turned off the roundabout at Heathfield, along Bovey straits, and upwards towards Dartmoor, passing the Edge Moor Hotel, and turning left at the next junction.

The steep climb up to the moor was one he knew well, and there was no other traffic about, apart from the seven struggling cyclists he had passed on the steep incline, who were by now some distance behind.

He reached the peak of the hill and headed towards Princetown, which was clearly signposted.

Looking to his right he was able to see the tops of Hounds Tor, and the impending junction.

His mind briefly flashed back to when he was last here, on that cold bleak, misty morning, some years ago, weapons in hand.

Four hundred metres later, he pulled over on the left, in the open unsheltered car park, suitable for about three cars, on a good day.

Turning the engine off, he took a deep breath in, and got out walking around to the boot. Reaching in, he pulled out his tattered old waterproof jacket. As he did, he looked around to see if there was anyone else around. Happy that there wasn't anyone, he slipped the musty smelling coat on, and took out a woollen beanie hat from the pocket. Pulling it down on his head, he covered his ears and pulled the collar of the jacket up. Then he slammed the boot of the car down, ensuring it had locked properly, then remotely locking the car, crossed the road, and climbed over the small locked wooden gate.

Having walked a small distance into the thick tussock grass, he paused and got his bearings. The information about the Burns brothers' location meant that Reuben's approach was hidden from view, both from the road, gate, and observation point he was going to reach. Standing up, he shivered slightly the dampness in the air, and low mist made for a chilly morning. Looking down at his Suunto 9 peak GPS watch, he pressed a button on the side which brought up the route he had already tapped in. It showed a little over 400m until he reached the point which on paper suggested the best observation point. Turning slightly right he started pacing out the 400m. The route he had chosen kept him in a small re-entrant hidden from view, until he turned and started the small gradual climb to the top of the bank. Before his head would be visible, he dropped to all fours, and crept forward for about five metres, adopting a prone position as he reached the crest. The grass was about twelve inches in hight but was dry underfoot. Rolling on to his left side, he reached into his breast pocket and took out a small but powerful set of binoculars, which he had bought many years ago for his Royal Marine's sniper course, and they had served him well. As old and battered as they were, you'd be lucky to get a better pair, even with today's advancements.

Propping himself up on his elbows, he looked down into the small group of farm buildings ahead of him in the valley. He estimated that they were about six hundred metres away. The view was unobstructed, and the location, within the re-entrant protected it from wind, and the elements.

In his mind, Reuben had already decided that this was the point, not only for what he planned but from where to execute it. There was no going back, despite every fibre in his body telling him to walk away and enjoy retirement with Sarah. Reuben tensed, and he narrowed his eyes, squinting into the eyepieces. There were figures coming out of the main farm building. Adjusting the focus, he counted five figures, all male, all smoking. Unmistakably there were two who stood out, above the others, literally. It was the Burns brothers! Reuben had imprinted their faces in his memory the very first time he had met them. He could see that they engaged in an animated conversation, and both were wearing dirty white vests. Their arms and hands appeared filthy as though they had been working on machinery or similar. Finding them had sealed his decision, and the plan was evolving in his head.

CHAPTER THIRTY-NINE

Sarah was none the wiser when Reuben returned home later that day. He explained that he had decided to do a bit of map reading, and had gone up to the area of Princetown, which in fact wasn't far from the truth. Sarah seemed happy with that and didn't give it another thought.

It was Saturday morning; Reuben was sat in the lounge with the curtains and blinds half drawn. Sarah walked in and plonked herself down in the wing-backed chair opposite. They were incredibly happy in their own company, and spent many hours just sat together, reading chatting, and sharing their meals. Neither felt it necessary to inform the other of their daily plans or movements unless they had made specific plans. Sarah would be driving to the superstore on Topsham Road, a weekly expedition.

Reuben left in his car about ten minutes before Sarah, and headed off in the direction of East Devon, starting the journey that could not be stopped, and putting into place the plan that would change so many lives forever.

The journey along the A3052 towards the Jurassic Close coastline was trouble free, for a Saturday. He recalled all those years ago, where his frequent journeys to Seaton Police Station was often held up, because of a tractor, or caravan, but not today.

He arrived at his destination in about forty minutes, and pulled into the parking area, which at once became familiar, and bought back many memories. His was the only car there, and turned the ignition off, and sat staring out ahead of him. His mind and heart raced, as he tumbled over all the pros and cons, which were quickly swept to one side together with any emotional rationale.

Getting out of the car he walked over to the wooden gate and climbed over it. Having done so he stood still and listened intently. Happy that he was alone, he entered the overgrown area, and recalled the precise approach to the shallow pit he had dug all those years ago. He counted his paces down and was stood beside the exact spot within a noticeably short time. He had done an excellent job. It was hidden from view, and there was no sign that anyone, or thing had been poking around in the area, and the ground looked undisturbed. Reuben squatted down and cleared the stinging nettles that had grown to one side with his foot and assessed the ground. There was a waft of wild garlic. Standing up he grinned and walked back to the car, no stopping now. Having climbed back over the gate, he went to the rear of the car, opened the boot, and before reaching in, paused, and looked around. He was still on his own. He reached in a pulled out the folded trench shovel, a curio he had bought from a military show several years before. A handy bit of kit to keep in the car; you never know when you would need something like it. Closing the boot quietly he vaulted the gate and returned to the shallow pit. Scything the now extended tool, he swept away the grass nettles and small branches and lowered himself onto his knees. Pausing he glanced up and listened. Nothing. He began to dig in slow movements, discarding the compacted soil to one side, but out of sight of anyone that would have been passing, conscious he would be needing it again the following days. Within only a few minutes his compact spade hit the hard object buried beneath. Pausing to look around, Reuben listened intently but heard nothing apart from the buzzard and two crows, high above in the sky, fighting for dominance.

Kneeling, he leant forward and scraped the loose soil away, revealing the tightly wrapped bin liners, bound with yards of gaffer tape.

Pulling it out he cradled it and stood up. The package appeared untouched and like it had been buried the day before. He held the package in his right hand and bent down to pick up the spade in his left. Turning, he walked to the edge of the undergrowth on to the path and turned to look back to where he had been. Apart from the foliage, which was slightly flattened, you couldn't tell anyone had been there, and you couldn't see where he had been digging. The flattened foliage and nettles would rise again.

Pausing again he could see that the route back to the car was clear, and it was still quiet. Taking a deep breath, he walked back to the car. He closed the boot with a thud and slid into the driver's seat.

Closing the door, he looked into his rear-view mirror, and took a deep breath of air in, exhaling slowly. Then he started the car, and selecting first gear started the journey, which would change many lives forever.

CHAPTER FORTY

Reuben had planned the day carefully. He had gone online earlier in the week and noted that am army unit was live firing across most of Dartmoor's live firing ranges that week as a prelude to a major European exercise the following month. This meant that he could do what he wanted within a five-day time slot. Less time for inquisitive observations or questions from members of the public.

He drove towards the eastern boundary of Merryvale ranges, and his research had shown that there was no one on it today despite the red flags being posted. This was a range he knew well from his snipers course all those years ago. He arrived at the pull-in next to a five-bar gate at the eastern side of the range.

Reuben's journey from East Devon to the top of Dartmoor was uneventful and seemed to go on forever, when in fact it was probably an hour and ten minutes.

Pulling over to the rough cut into the granite and chalk bank was simple but allowed the car to be off the road, and not cause an obstruction.

Rueben got out of the car and, standing up, took his phone out from his door pocket, and looked at the screen. Full power but no signal. *Well there's a change,* he thought, and smiled to himself. It was the same with the old military radios they used to use, useless.

He paused, dropped the phone back into the door pocket, and

stood up, straining to listen to the distant sounds of mortars and high velocity rounds in the distance.

"Perfect," he murmured.

Closing the door slowly, he went to the rear and opened the boot. Picking up his trusty old Barbour jacket, it revealed the muddied bin liners. Zipping the jacket up, he felt the colder breeze coming off the moor, where the weather could change without warning trapping many a seasoned tourist.

Bundle under his arm, collar up, he closed the boot and within a matter of seconds had locked the car and climbed the fence, walking on the small gravel track away from the road.

Within about ten minutes, the road was a good distance away, and he had passed several MOD signs warning against trespassing and reminding persons of the live-firing area.

A flapping sound made him look up, and he dropped to his knees. The red hoisted range flag fluttered with the breeze that had built up in such a fleeting time. Reuben rose and walked to the base of the flag and sat on the flag stones which surrounded it.

Laying the weapon across his lap he began the lengthy process of unwrapping it carefully, so that the wrappings could be used again. As each bin liner was removed, he tucked it carefully within the stone supports; it made for not only a good marker point, but also a good reference point should the weather close in later. Although he reckoned that he only needed thirty minutes or so, in and out.

He removed the weapon from the case, and loaded ten rounds into the detached magazine, stuffing into his right-hand jacket pocket.

The final bag covered the case, and he slid it under the second layer of stone, where he was able to hide it totally.

Removing the front and rear lens caps, he held the beautifully engineered scope to his right eye and stared out into the haze ahead of him. It was remarkable that the clarity and ease of movement on the dials was as if it was brand new. Again, the smell of rifle oil was hypnotic, and he took it all in.

Looking down at the bracket and slider for the scope on top of the rifle, he could see the small almost invisible marks for the zeroed scope mount, etched in all those years ago by Margot's husband. Lining them up, he tightened the two knurled knobs on the sliding plate, securing it into place. Reuben had guessed that his mission's target range would not require hours and hours of firing and adjustment, as he had done on his Royal Marines sniper course, He was going to be as close as he could so that he accomplish his goal as quickly and cleanly as possible.

Placing the magazine under the body of the rifle, he eased the leather strap to one side, and pushed upwards, hearing the satisfying click as the magazine was secure. Standing up, he cradled the weapon in his folded arms, and walked towards an area which was about 200 metres in a Westerly direction.

As proven from the course all those years ago, he knew that each 100 metres accounted for 110 of his steps, and that if he maintained the direction, it would take him to a firing point which was used by snipers from all around the world on a regular basis, but not this week.

The firing point seemed to appear out of nowhere, and it was almost exactly where his steps finished.

Kneeling, Reuben leant the weapon up against the marker post, and took his Barbour off, laying it down with the outside of it on the floor, and spread out. He lay down on his front and propped himself up on his elbows looking towards the various manufactured earth banks, ahead of him. The nearest was 300m and the furthest was 600m. The design was such that to engage all the targets set at different ranges would involve little movement on behalf of the shooter, and their weapon. Approximately midway was another range flag, which had been hoisted the previous day. The flag was an invaluable indicator of the wind's strength and direction. Nowadays it is all calculated with up-to-date mechanical devices, with calibrations in handheld books. In Reuben's day careful analysis of vegetation and trees was always an effective way, especially when waiting for when the wind would drop.

Today there was the odd breeze, which would cause the flag to flutter for a brief time, nothing to worry about with this sort of rifle at about 400 metres. The sounds of the mortars being fired several miles away was continuous and would continue for the rest of the day, which meant there would be nobody on the sniper range but him.

Reuben was right-handed and, leaning across, brought the gleaming weapon down to his right and pushed out in front. Resting the butt on the jacket of his coat, he cradled the stock having entwined his left wrist in the supple yet taut sling. If he hadn't known better, the weapon felt like it had been set up for him, with no requirements for adjustments. Holding the cocking handle between his right thumb and forefinger, he raised it and bought it back whilst ensuring he could see the mechanism gram the base of the first round and hold it before the bolt was pushed forward in a smooth action, chambering the round in the barrel. Releasing the grip on his right hand he pulled the safety catch backwards, making the rifle ready to fire. Replacing the grip, he ensured his trigger finger remained on the outside of the trigger guard. He squirmed until he was comfortable resting on both elbows, his right leg drawn up. Theoretically the straight line of the rifle should continue so an invisible line cut through the centre of the prone body. He was comfortable enough to maintain it for an extended period.

He closed his left eye and adjusted his head so that the sight picture was clear, and not obstructed, and not close enough to hurt his eye when the trigger was pulled (an injury laughably known as snipers' eye).

Reuben settled on the 400-metre mound, where he could clearly see the wooden frame that would hold all manner of targets on a normal day. He decided to use the right-hand upright frame as his target. It was a simple piece of four-by-two timber with a small natural knot in it. This was the target for today.

Reuben let the weapon rest on his extended left arm and held the butt tight into his shoulder and right cheek bone adjusting his body slightly until the crosshair in the sight settled on the base of the knot in the wood. He closed his eyes, and inhaled slowly, held it then exhaled just as slow. Repeating this two more times, he inhaled again, held it, and opened his eyes. He was pleased to see the crosshairs on the knot in the wood.

Seeing that the flag was hanging loose, he gently curled his finger on the trigger, and repeated the process. As he held his breath he increased the pressure, and the weapon jarred as the high velocity round sped towards the knot in the wood. Looking through the scope, he saw the wood splinter almost immediately in the middle of the intended target. Spot on!

Reuben winced. He had forgotten to put his small ear defenders in, and his ears rung with a high-pitched squeal, which made him look up, squinting as the ringing subsided.

Fuck that was loud, he thought as the sound of the shot echoed around and beyond his position. As he pulled the action back, slowly, he caught the empty cylinder, before it went flying off. A trick he learnt as to not reveal the firer's position later. Little did he know how it would become so important less that twenty-four hours later.

Having placed the two small ear defenders in his ears, he repeated the shooting process five times. The resultant grouping on the target was remarkable, not only for the un-zeroed weapon, but also regarding the skillset that he had not lost from all those years ago. From start to finish the whole episode had taken less than five minutes. Ensuring he had all five empty cylinders, he gathered all his bits and pieces, put his coat on, and walked briskly back to his vehicle, with ears still ringing and the almost seductive smell of cordite in his nostrils. He stayed at the first drop site, rewrapping the rifle for about a further thirty minutes and disguising any evidence of his presence before climbing the fence and placing the rifle in the car boot under the musky jacket.

Sitting in the car, he gripped the steering wheel hard, and pushed himself back into the seat, closing his eyes, and taking in what he had just done and, more importantly, what he was about to do.

Reaching down, he turned the ignition key, engaged first gear and moved out of the parking bay, looking over his shoulder as he went. He drove onto the tarmac, towards Haytor, and his destiny.

CHAPTER FORTY-ONE

The Burns brothers had risen early from their alcohol-fuelled late night at the isolated farmhouse. Today they had made no plans, and the rogues' gallery of guests over the last week had all gone.

Each room was a mess, with discarded cans and bottles, along with overflowing ashtrays.

The smell of the smoke, and unwashed bodies, permeated from the farmhouse into the courtyard, and beyond. The pile of dirty clothes had risen in the outhouse beside the broken washing machine.

Cleanliness was a forgotten word within the group, and was reflected in the colour of the bedding, or what was left of the bedding. Their mattresses in each of their rooms, were stained and infested with armies of creepy crawlies, and other unwelcome guests.

Michael walked into the open courtyard, where Thomas was sat. The old Rattan furniture set was rusty, and thread bare but served a purpose, surrounding the cold fire pit, which was full of cigarette butts and empty tins.

Thomas turned to his brother and stifled a yawn.

"We need to finish this, it's dragging on."

Michael leant forward and lit a cigarette that he had been holding, offering his sibling one from a packet, which was eagerly taken. He passed the cigarette, which was used to light the offering.

"Yep, we do, that's for sure, but we need to be careful. They aren't stupid, and I don't trust this lot down here."

"Maybe leave it at that."

Michael's comment to his brother almost made Thomas choke.

"Don't you ever say that, ever, do you understand?" Michael jolted back, not expecting his brother's barking reply, and it was loud enough to be heard beyond the walls of the farmhouse, and down the small valley where they were.

Reuben had returned home the previous night just before it got too dark and had left the rifle and all the other pieces of equipment in the boot of the car under the trusty coat.

Sarah, had left a note on the lounge table, saying that she was going to her sister's, for a catch-up, in Horsham, West Sussex, but would only be there for one night despite the journey taking about three hours. He estimated that she would return at about teatime the next day at the latest, making his plans even more straightforward than he'd imagined, without the need to explain to Sarah his long absences during these two days. After the kisses at the end of the small note there was a PS informing him that there was a quiche and salad plated up in the fridge for him. He smiled.

Cleared the windscreen night, turning things over in his head, time and time again. He decided to get up at about 04:00, and showered straight away, putting on the same clothes he had worn the previous day. Within an hour he had had a bowl of porridge scattered with brown sugar, two cups of sweet tea, and a digestive biscuit which he took with him as he walked to the car. Munching away as he lifted the boot open, and glanced inside, seeing that the coat was undisturbed. Closing the boot, he pushed the rest of the biscuit in his mouth and got into the car. Starting the engine, he cleared the windows, and pulled out on to the main road, and started his journey towards Haytor.

CHAPTER FORTY-TWO

Reuben decided to drive to the main car park below and to the left of the imposing Tor, popular with many, both locally and tourists alike. He himself had been there many times, not only as a visitor, but also when undertaking fast rope access with the Firearms teams, which always appeared to attract the crowds.

He would skirt the low stone wall which disappeared away from the main road, and up the small hill out of sight. The farm and its outbuildings were easily visible beyond the hill and out of sight of prying eyes. The small hill and layout of the land with gullies, and re-entrants, would stifle the retort of the rifle should he use it.

The car park was thankfully empty, and there was a chill in the air; the clock on the dashboard displayed 0510hrs, perfect!

Reuben opened the boot and put the coat on. Leaving it open he grabbed the rifle, and magazine, and closing the boot, locked the car, and jogged over towards the dry-stone wall, beneath the proverbial bushy topped tree. He knelt and slung the weapon over his left shoulder, turned to his right and started the climb up the slope, keeping tight to the wall on his left. It was only a matter of ten minutes before he reached the brow of the hill. Reuben lay the rifle down on the damp grass and lay down next to it. Edging forward, he kept his head down and pushed the heather to one side. Looking ahead of him he saw that laying nicely in the re-entrant was the small farm layout. It was a farm which was out of view from the main road, and accessed by a muddy, and unkept track, with broken archaic wooden gates at the entrance from the road, and at 100 metres from the house. Apart from the small main run-down farmhouse, there were several outbuildings all in a state of disrepair, and bang in the middle at an awkward angle was the grey Vauxhall Insignia.

Reaching inside his jacket Reuben took out his aged and trusted binoculars and resting on his elbows he focused on the farmhouse. As he looked at the building his mind reached back to both his sniper's course and time on the Firearms teams. The number of times he had had to colour code, and count off windows and doors, or draw pictures of buildings and locations. Today, remarkably, conditions could not have been better. There was a wisp of smoke drifting out of the small chimney stack, a good sign that there were people in there and that the conditions for an exact shot were perfect, and he smiled to himself.

He could not see anyone in either the windows or doorways, and the misted windows on the car would suggest it had not been moved recently, certainly not through the night before, as the mud to the rear of the car had not been driven on since the overnight rain.

Placing the binoculars on the ground in front of him, he stared intently ahead. There were several tried and tested ways to estimate distances to targets, but at the same time there are limits, and things to consider. Nowadays, the Services have electrical, and computerised equipment, but Reuben was used to the old methods, which if done correctly are foolproof.

Distance to objects can be difficult to judge if you are looking downhill, or uphill, whether you are looking through cover, or over dips in the ground or valleys, and hot weather can distort an exact assessment.

Different methods that can be used are often decided when

taking in all the conditions, and more importantly, how great the distance is.

Sometimes several methods can be used, and Reuben had decided that this is what he would do.

As he looked the ground before him, it dropped, going downhill. He estimated that he could fit four football fields in the gap between him and the centre of the house. He also bracketed it, inasmuch as he knew it was more than 300m and no more than 500m. He was happy that the figure he came to each time was 400m. At the distance if he was out a little it wouldn't matter a great deal, and if the weather remained as it was, he could deliver a fatal torso shot without the need for any adjustments, from when he test fired it the previous day. Suddenly a movement in the doorway made him reach for his binoculars, and his heart raced. He watched as a tall male left the door and walked towards what appeared to be a firepit in the yard, only a small distance from the porch. He sat down and lit a cigarette.

Reuben smiled. "Gotcha," he hissed recognising the dishevelled figure as one of the twins, Thomas. He dropped the binoculars and brought the rifle up to his shoulder. As he did, he removed the magazine and double-checked he had put the five rounds in it. Happy with this, he pulled back on the bolt, loading the first round into the chamber, and ensured the safety catch was on.

He adopted the classic right-handed prone position with his right leg bent at the knee, propped up on his elbows, continually watching the figure sat below him.

Looking through the high precision scope, which he had left on, he studied the figure, and placed the gradated crosshairs on the twin's right cheek. He could see that the wind was still, and it was quiet.

Glancing down at his watch on his left wrist he noted it was 0610hrs, and the sun was rising. He was happy that his position was good, and that no one could see him from anywhere around.

As he adjusted his position, and slowed his breathing, he saw the second figure leave the porch, with an unlit cigarette in his mouth, walking towards the seated figure. He sat beside him and leant over so that he could light his smoke as well.

Reuben knew that the second male was the other twin, and that it was now or never.

Suddenly Reuben heard Thomas shout at his brother, but could not hear what was said, but it was loud enough to be heard at a range of 400m.

Reuben had slowed the breathing rate right down despite his heart racing.

The crosshairs had not moved; as he breathed, the sight picture remained still.

Reuben's right thumb eased the safety catch at the rear of the sight upwards, making the weapon ready to fire. He would take out the brothers where they sat.

Suddenly Thomas stood up, took a long drag on his cigarette, and flicked it into the firepit. He turned to his brother as Reuben lost the sight picture. Michael abruptly stood up and took a step towards his brother. They were arguing, and Reuben moved the sight right, he placed it on the back of Michael's head as he faced his brother, causing Thomas's head to be level but obscured.

Reuben's forefinger tightened on the crafted trigger, and he held his breath. His heart was beating hard, he could feel it thumping his chest, and pounding his temples. The rifle jumped slightly as the weapon fired; the crosshairs returned immediately back to where he had aimed. It was odd, he didn't hear the snap and crack as the pin struck the round sending it at high velocity to the targets less than a second away.

Michael was not happy at the way Thomas had spoken, or rather yelled, at him, and his brother standing up so abruptly was a threat he was not prepared to put up with. He stood up and stepped towards him thrusting his face into his brother's who turned to face him.

Neither would have heard the rifle 400m away as it let loose the 7.62mm round towards them. In less than half a second, as Michael opened his mouth to speak, the round entered the back of his head, travelling at 760 metres per second. The round emptied his skull spraying his brother Thomas, before exiting his right eye socket. It had altered course and had started to tumble hitting Thomas at the base of his nose and taking off all his head above the jaw. Brothers who had come into this world together, left it together. Both were dead before their crumpled bodies hit the fire pit, tipping the contents onto the courtyard.

Reuben watched as the heads exploded in a fine red mist.

He quickly re-cocked the rifle, ejecting the spent cartridge, and placed his sight on to the slumped bodies. He knew instinctively that the cold shot had dispatched the two at the same time. Neither of them could have survived the catastrophic damage the shot had caused. Applying the safety catch, he turned on to his left side, removed the magazine, and pulled back on the bolt. The unfired round spun out and away from the breech into the heather bush about eighteen inches away to his right. "Bollocks!" Reuben swore.

Looking down at the farm, he saw that the brothers had not moved.

Job done, he thought. *That was for my friends.*

Despite digging around and tugging at the bush he could not find either the spent round, or unfired round, he did not have time to spend at the firing point.

Reluctantly he gathered up everything, but as hard as he looked, he could not find the two rounds from the rifle. He crawled back below the crest, stood up turned and went back to the car. As he walked back beside the wall, he could see that there were still no cars, or people in the area. Letting out a sigh of relief, he continued down, cursing the fact he could not find the empty cylinder. If he had done that on any of the stalks and shoots on the sniper course, he would have failed.

He decided to go straight home, avoiding the trip to East Devon, to replace the Rifle and ancillaries. Arriving at home less that forty-five minutes later, it was clear that none of his neighbours had risen. He and his 'special' package slipped into the house unnoticed.

Reuben had decided to hide the rifle in his garage, a place Sarah never entered. He would stash it safely and securely amongst discarded rolls of carpet that had lain in there for ages until things had quietened down in the future.

Having done this, he hung his waterproof jacket in his shed, and went and showered before making a long awaited cup of morning Earl Grey tea.

Sat in the lounge, he sipped and thought about what he had done. He was adamant that what he had done was what his mates who were no longer with him would have done. He knew that it was the twins who had murdered his mates, his best mates, and his raised his cup up towards the ceiling.

"Cheers."

CHAPTER FORTY-THREE

The bodies were found later that day, by an anonymous person who rang 999.

Police descended upon the scene in droves, and a murder investigation began at once.

To be fair, although greeted by a macabre scene, most agreed that they deserved it, and there was little sympathy.

Rumours quickly spread of a "professional" hit, possibly by a rival gang.

During the search, their phones, and laptops were seized, and hours and hours of examination revealed evidence and communication linking them to the deaths of the police officers, and communication implicating them in the deaths of the two women all those years ago.

As this information came to light within the incident room, the effort in finding those responsible waned. The media initially were all over it, with wild thoughts, and exuberant scenarios. They reported wildly on the links to all the murders, and the public feedback was not sympathetic. The case was closed after a relatively brief time, with no apparent objections, apart from the brothers' family.

CHAPTER FORTY-FOUR

Reuben and Sarah had followed the killing of the two brothers like everyone else, but as with the rest of the public, Sarah had no sympathy.

There had been times when Reuben had been slightly nervous when announcements in the first stages had mentioned "leads" or different theories.

About six months later, Reuben was sat in his lounge; Sarah was out, as normal at another coffee meeting with her friends.

He was watching the recent series of *Commando* on the TV which he had recorded, and watched several times, when his doorbell rang. Pausing the TV, he stood up stretched, and went to the front door where he could see a tall shadowy figure through the glass.

He opened the door, and was pleased to see it was Simon, who had been one of his team members through those glory days and was still serving.

They embraced and both felt the emotion of missing each other and lost friends. Patting Simon's back, Reuben stepped back.

"Come in. Come in."

Wiping his feet, Simon walked in and closed the door behind him.

Entering the lounge, Simon pointed at the paused picture.
"Really?"

Reuben shrugged. "Old habits."

"Please sit down," he added and pointed to the single chair. "Drink?"

"No thanks," came the reply as he sat down and crossed his legs.

Reuben said, "Great to see you mate, how does being a Detective Inspector on crime suit you?"

Simon shrugged.

"Good money, long hours, stress. Apart from that…" They laughed.

"Reuben I've been the SIO, on the Haytor double murder." Reuben sat up and leant forward.

"How's it going."

"No one really gives a shit if I'm honest." He went on to say that that evidence was sufficient to link them to the murders.

"I miss the lads, good lads, with all that training, what a waste."

Reuben nodded. There was a silence. Simon then looked at Reuben intently.

"You have no views either way mate?"

"No not really, not going to lose any sleep about it."

Simon cleared his throat.

"You'd tell me if you knew something; you'd say, wouldn't you?"

Reuben looked shocked.

"Why would you say that?"

Simon explained that every surviving member of the team was being spoken to including himself.

Reuben relaxed. "No mate, I don't know shit, but deep down I thought it was those twats, gut feeling you know."

Simon nodded. He paused.

"We had something special, didn't we?"

Reuben nodded, picturing all the boys. Phil, Mike, Tim, Rick, Jason and Brian. Throwing biscuits around, pissing around with kit, spraying CS under toilet doors... it went on and on.

Simon stood up pulling his jacket straight.

"I'll leave you mate, things to do people to see."

Reuben walked him to the door and opened it. As he stepped over the threshold he turned and offered his hand, as Reuben took it he felt a small matchbox-sized box in his palm.

"Reuben, I love you like a brother; we all do, take care," Simon said as he stared at him and smiled.

Shaking his hand Simon walked out onto the main road out of sight. Reuben was taken aback and felt he should have said something.

Looking down he shook the box. There was something in there, but it made no sound. Closing the door, he went and sat back down in the lounge.

Carefully opening the small plain box, he could see two wrapped cylindrical items, one slightly longer than the other at about four inches.

He opened the shorter one, both were wrapped in tissue paper.

He unwrapped it, the paper dropped to the floor, and he felt the tears welling up. He placed the item in his lap and with shaking hands unwrapped the second and longer one.

Holding both, one in each hand he started to cry, and the crying turned into sobbing, while the items fell on to the carpet. Reuben cupped his head in his hands as he wept like never before. The tears ran down his nose and through his fingers onto the carpet and splashed onto the unfired round and empty cylinder on the floor at his feet.